THE HISTORY OF JANE DOE

Michael Belanger

PENGUIN BOOKS

PENGUIN BOOKS

An imprint of Penguin Random House LLC, New York

First published in the United States of America by Dial Books
Published by Penguin Books, an imprint of Penguin Random House LLC, 2019

Visit us online at penguinrandomhouse.com

THE LIBRARY OF CONGRESS HAS CATALOGED THE DIAL BOOKS EDITION AS FOLLOWS:
Names: Belanger, Michael, author.
Title: The history of Jane Doe / Michael Belanger.
Description: New York, NY : Dial Books, [2018] | Summary: "After his girlfriend commits suicide, a teenage history buff looks back at their relationship and tries to understand what lead to the tragedy" —Provided by publisher.
Identifiers: LCCN 2017054139| ISBN 9780735228818 (hardcover) | ISBN 9780735228832 (ebook)
Subjects: | CYAC: Coming of age—Fiction. | Suicide—Fiction. | Dating (Social customs)—Fiction. | Depression, Mental—Fiction. | Mothers and sons—Fiction.
Classification: LCC PZ7.1.B4457 His 2018 | DDC [Fic]—dc23
LC record available at https://lccn.loc.gov/2017054139

Penguin Books ISBN 9780735228825

Printed in the United States of America

10 9 8 7 6 5 4 3 2 1

For Mary, Jack, and Hammy

"If you think you're going to sum up your whole life on this little bit of paper, you're crazy."

—Jane's Fortune Cookie

61 DAYS AFTER

JANE DOE

I don't have cancer and both of my parents are still alive. I just thought I'd get that out of the way so you're not disappointed. While we're at it, I might as well tell you that I'm not a vampire, I don't have magical powers, and the closest I've ever come to fighting a war against an evil dystopian government was in a video game.

Now that you're no longer expecting a story about orphaned vampires fighting an oligarchy of terminally ill wizards—although come to think of it, that does sound pretty cool—I'll tell you why I'm writing this. It's not to "document my feelings" or "look for self-destructive patterns," like my therapist, Rich, suggested. I guess you could say I'm a history buff, but don't worry, this isn't a story about the Civil War or little houses on the prairie. History has enough stories already, things way more interesting than anything I could make up—the epic battles, rumors about people playing games with severed human heads, all of the unsolved mysteries involving rocks and ritual sacrifices. I know people say history repeats itself, I just hope I'm not around when it does.

The truth is, I'm writing this mostly to help me understand everything that happened over the past year between my (ex) girlfriend Jane and me. When you read as much history as I do, you start to wish real life also had textbooks, the kind with illustrated chronologies and "Did You Know?" sections that make everything so simple and easy to understand. Any good historian knows that the past is a lot more complex than cause-and-effect charts and corny acronyms make it out to be; but Jane, a person more complicated than any revolution, more confusing than any war, and more life changing than any invention—and I'm including the lightbulb and chocolate chip cookies when I say that—deserves her own volume. And so, in a way, I guess you could say I'm writing one for her.

Since she's been gone, I've been scouring documents, text messages, her bizarre drawings inspired by the boredom of biology—anything to help me shine a light on the history of Jane. The only obstacle has been my mom, who has started checking on me every hour to either annoy me or make sure I'm still alive.

As if on cue, I hear her walk down the hallway, the wooden floorboards creaking as she makes her way to my room. She knocks lightly, and when I don't answer, her knocks become more aggressive.

"Dinner's ready," she says through the door. She jiggles the doorknob.

"It's locked," I say, just because I know it will irritate her.

She hovers outside the room, a presence more terrifying than anything found in a horror movie: a mother who has dinner ready.

"Are you coming down?" she asks.

"Yup," I say. "Right after I finish summoning Lucifer."

"What?"

"Can you bring me my dinner like I'm a prisoner?"

I hear her footsteps recede down the hallway. She sighs as she goes.

I know I'm being a jerk, but I can't just smile and pretend everything's okay. Even though I know that's what everyone wants.

Before I forget, I should tell you that everything I'm about to write is true. It's not one of those made-up stories that has morals and plot devices and well-crafted metaphors. History doesn't have room for all that. Facts are facts, whether you like them or not. I'm only changing one name: hers. It just didn't feel right to use her real name, so I'm calling her Jane, as in Jane Doe.

67 DAYS AFTER

BURGERVILLE

I live in the sprawling, barely suburban wasteland of Williamsburg. No, not the Williamsburg where people wear funny hats
and visit old buildings. That one's in Virginia and was named
after King William III, affectionately referred to as King Billy
and admired for his work in the Glorious Revolution—otherwise
known as the most boring revolution in the history of the world,
a sort of happily-ever-after fairy tale where hardly anyone got
decapitated and the king gave everyone their rights. Nice to live
through, boring to read about.

I'm not talking about the Williamsburg in Brooklyn either,
where people dress in tight pants, point out the irony of the mod-
ern condition, and, well, wear funny hats. That Williamsburg was
named after Colonel John Williams, a revolutionary war veteran
who bears an uncanny resemblance to Jabba the Hutt.

I'm referring to the lesser-known Williamsburg of Connecticut, home of that guy who knew a guy who had a cousin who sat
next to (*insert famous celebrity*) on a bus. Our Williamsburg's name
comes from an unfortunate coincidence: the rise of the middle
class and, shortly later, the invention of the hamburger. Originally called Burgherville because the word *burgher* means middle

class, the town found itself the butt of too many jokes. Newspaper articles referred to the various neighborhoods of Burgherville as cuts of beef, extending from the Marrow outward to the Rump. People in the town were ranked according to their looks: well-done, rare, or if you were extremely unfortunate, ground beef. By the end of the 1950s, everyone was sick of it and the mayor called an emergency meeting to rename the town. At the time, the hero of Burgherville, a local football star named Frank Williams, had just been killed in a car accident. A motion was made to call the town Williamstown, at which point another council member, in probably his most important contribution to mankind, put the two words together, and so Williamsburg—albeit the *lesser* Williams-burg—was born.

Most of us still call it Burgerville, though, and spell it like it sounds.

When I told Jane that story she thought I was making it up. Her exact words were, "I feel like I'm in the Twilight Zone." But I think that's how Jane felt most of the time. Like she didn't really belong, no matter where she was.

254 DAYS BEFORE

NOW YOU'RE IN KANSAS

I first saw Jane a little under a year ago, in biology. Mr. Parker was explaining the difference between RNA and DNA, using visual aids that depicted each as a superhero, when the door slowly opened. The girl standing in the doorway looked lost. Not in the sense that she didn't know if she was in the right class, but lost in general. Seeing all of our heads turned to the doorway, Mr. Parker stopped his lecture and nodded, like he'd been waiting the entire class for this moment.

"There you are," he said excitedly, but it sounded over-the-top, kind of like the way people talk to their dogs. "Class, we have a new student. This is Jane Doe." On the screen in the front of the room, Mr. Parker had left a picture of a strand of RNA wearing a cape and tights with the caption: *Quick, DNA needs our help!* Jane turned to the screen and looked back at the class, as if to say, *What kind of school is this?*

"You can sit anywhere you like," Mr. Parker said, before realizing there was only one empty seat in the class—right next to me. The confused look on Jane's face gave way to a sinister smile, like we had an inside joke. She nodded and began walking toward me, my heart racing as she approached.

My mind became a camera, cataloguing every detail of the mysterious stranger as she made her way to the desk. Her pale face was framed by long black hair streaked with red, which may not sound that weird to you, but for Burgerville she might as well have had *666* stamped on her forehead. As she brushed a few strands of hair out of her eyes, I noticed her nails were painted all different colors. When she reached the halfway point, we locked eyes and I had to immediately look away; something about the way she looked at me made me feel like she could read my mind. As she got closer and I began to seriously consider using my lunch bag to stop myself from hyperventilating, I worked up the courage to look at her again. A black T-shirt hung loosely around her body and bracelets covered her wrists. The name of a band I'd never heard of—Pineapple Melody—was inscribed above a pineapple-shaped guitar, the slogan *Folk You* scrawled beneath. By the time I scanned all the way down to her shoes—heavy black leather boots with neon-green laces—she had already taken her seat.

Mr. Parker then began to ask her a series of questions, which always makes me really uncomfortable, but it didn't seem to faze Jane at all. Really, Mr. Parker was the one who seemed uncomfortable.

"What brings you to Williamsburg?" he asked, his cheery voice blunted by Jane's somber expression.

"My parents are punishing me," she said.

Mr. Parker looked around, unsure how to proceed. Then, as if reading from a book of common English phrases, he robotically asked, "Where are you from?"

"The Williamsburg in Brooklyn," she said. "I guess my parents thought it was ironic."

"That's quite a coincidence," Mr. Parker said, struggling to keep a smile on his face. "How do you like our town so far?"

"Can it really be called a town?" she asked.

Mr. Parker gulped. "What are your interests? Remember, this is biology." He laughed uncomfortably as the class continued to stare.

"Folk music and conspiracy theories."

The class began to whisper. Mr. Parker held up his hand for silence.

"That's . . ." He struggled to find the right word before finally settling on *interesting*. "Very interesting," he repeated, sounding relieved now that the interview was almost over. "And is there anything else you'd like the class to know about you? Maybe something you did this summer?"

Jane paused to think. "I visited Mount Rushmore."

"I love Mount Rushmore," Mr. Parker said, happy to be on familiar ground. "What'd you think?"

"It's amazing that these rocks somehow look exactly like the presidents. Kind of spooky when you think about it."

I laughed, then quickly caught it. Mr. Parker didn't seem to get the joke. Same for pretty much everyone else in the class.

"Oh," Mr. Parker said. "I could see why you'd think that, but Mount Rushmore is actually manmade. It was finished in . . ." He snapped his fingers, trying to remember the date. "Help me out here, Ray."

My reputation for history was well-known, but I didn't see this one coming. It was like I'd suddenly entered a TV show. I cleared my throat. "1941," I said. "But I'm pretty sure she was being sarcastic, Mr. Parker."

I glanced at Jane. She mouthed *thank you*. I was so nervous I couldn't even attempt to move my lips.

"Of course," Mr. Parker said, forcing a laugh. "I was being sarcastic too." But I don't think anyone believed him. After a moment of awkward silence, he loosened his collar and said, "Well Jane, welcome to Williamsburg, or as we like to call it, Burgerville." At which point he proceeded to give a speech about how much she would like it, how friendly the people were, how he definitely understood sarcasm, and if there was anything she needed to just let him know.

But I could tell she wasn't really listening. Instead, she took out a notebook and started to draw. I looked at her desk and watched as she created an idyllic landscape with cows and chickens and for some reason, a minotaur. At the top of the page, two evil-looking eyes peered over the horizon like a sinister sunset. But my favorite part about it was the billboard in the background. It said:

Now You're in Kansas

Jane must have seen me looking at her, because as Mr. Parker continued his lecture about Captain RNA and DNA Man, she scribbled something in the margin of her notebook and slid it to the edge of her desk. *Is this place as weird as it seems?* it said.

I couldn't figure out which part of Burgerville she was referring to. The name? The other kids in class, all with the same exact outfit, what I'd come to think of as *Children of the Corn*–casual? Mr. Parker's strange comic book approach to science?

It was hard to know. For me, Burgerville had always occupied a gray area, a place where history meets one of those horribly depressing fairy tales. *Sort of*, I wrote in the corner of my notebook. We made eye contact once again and I thought my head might explode. As if she could hear my thoughts, Jane smiled and went back to finishing her drawing.

I turned to Mr. Parker and closed my eyes. As he continued to drone on about our genetic makeup, all I could think about was the mysterious stranger to my right.

88 DAYS AFTER

SIMON

Outside my window, I see an old oak tree. Its branches claw and scratch against the glass when the wind picks up. The sun is setting, the sky turning a bright shade of orange before an inky black creeps in from the horizon. A full moon sits at the edge of the sky, passive, an observer watching day turn into night.

The window, the tree, the moon. All roads lead back to Jane. History, the subject that used to feel so liberating, now feels suffocating, my year with Jane weighing down the present. Weighing down *me*.

"Ray," my mom yells from downstairs, "Simon's here."

Simon Blackburn and I have been best friends since middle school. Simon looks like your textbook definition of a nerd—think glasses and T-shirts that say things like *Does not play well with others.* But Simon's really not a nerd at all. He's terrible in math and knows next to nothing about comic books. His nerdiest attribute would have to be his love of vampire fiction, which is also the reason he used to occasionally wear fangs to school.

As Simon climbs the stairs, I try to muster up some happiness, a shred of the old Ray. If not a smile, then at least an expression that doesn't make it look like I'm constipated.

Simon makes his way down the hallway and peers into my room. "Ray? You okay?"

At first I'm slightly annoyed that concern and worry has become an appropriate conversation starter. Then I remember I'm sitting in the dark. In the corner of my room.

"I'm fine," I say.

Simon inches into the dark. I swivel my chair around to face him, realizing too late that I'm behaving an awful lot like an evil supervillain.

"Hi, Ray."

"Hi, Simon."

"So . . ."

These awkward pauses haven't always been there. The spaces Jane used to fill. We're still adjusting, recalibrating, waiting for time to shrink or expand or whatever it does.

Simon hits the light switch and automatically shields his eyes, a habit he picked up from reading too much vampire lit. "I can't believe tomorrow's the first day of senior year," he says.

"Don't remind me," I say. Another first day of school. Everyone's favorite day to show off new sneakers, industrial-grade binders, and pens that write in more than one color of ink. But what people forget is what happens after first days: second days and third days and fourth days. And Jane won't be there for any of them.

"Remember those shoes that light up when you walk?" Simon asks. "Well, I found an outlet in Canada that sells them in adult sizes. The website says they're coming back in style. You don't think Canada has different fashion than America, do you?"

"There are no borders when it comes to cool shoes," I say.

"That's what I thought," Simon says. He takes a seat on my bed and looks around the room, a barren landscape of my dirty laundry, plates riddled with crumbs, and open history books lying facedown on the ground, stuck on various episodes of Burgerville's history.

"Do you want me to pick you up tomorrow?" Simon asks, looking worried.

"I guess."

"Ray?"

"Simon?"

"Are you *sure* everything's okay?"

This time, I decide to take a different approach: I close my eyes and begin to snore.

"Okay, I know you don't have that disease where you immediately fall asleep"—Simon pauses—"or do you? And you've just been keeping it a secret from me this whole time?"

I open my eyes. "I don't have narcolepsy."

"Good to look on the bright side," Simon says. "That's the *worst* disease. Body parts literally fall right off."

"Um, Simon, you're thinking of leprosy," I say. I laugh and let my head fall back onto the chair. It must be the first time I've laughed in days. My cheeks hurt. Chest heavy. Those muscles haven't been getting much of a workout.

We make small talk for a little while, topics ranging from a weird dream Simon had where he was eating a gigantic mango— "But then I realized, it was me. I was the mango"—to Mr. Parker's recent pictures in the *Burgerville Gazette* dressed as Batman, then Simon stands up and tells me to get excited for the first day of senior year—mostly because we'll now be occupying the lunch tables closest to the dessert line.

"I'll do my best," I say.

Simon walks over to me and grabs my shoulder.

"I miss her too," he says. After an awkward pause, the moment heavy with all of the things we wish we could say but don't, Simon turns and walks away, almost tripping over a book about the colonial history of Burgerville as he makes his way out the door.

To be honest, I've never been the type of person to get excited about the first day of school, but now it's especially hard, even to fake it. Being around other people is difficult. Rich says I'm isolating myself, letting my "cognitive distortions" push people away. That's when I usually start zoning out, nodding politely as I visualize my next meal.

But still, it's good to see Simon, even if it's just to laugh for a little while. He's always been really good at cheering me up. It's a skill I credit to his family's history, a long lineage of people who had no choice but to look on the bright side and cash in on their shortcomings.

Simon's great-grandfather, for example, served in World War I until he fell in the first battle fought by Americans. And when I say fell, I mean he literally fell straight onto his bayonet. But that didn't stop him from becoming a war hero. No, sir. Because his impalement happened only a few seconds after the first shots were fired, he spent the rest of his life bragging to any reporter who would listen about his heroic exploits as the first American casualty of the Great War.

Simon's grandfather followed the war hero tradition and became a decorated Korean War veteran, famous for his heroic charge against a battalion of North Korean soldiers in the darkest days of the war. But it turns out most of his war stories weren't exactly true. First, he charged a group of *South* Korean soldiers. Whoops! And although the press reported him saying, "We will never surrender!" he actually screamed, "We surrender!" After people found out the truth, the government stripped him of all his war medals and he wrote a book chronicling his journey to infamy. It's called *From Hero to Zero: America's Most Hated Soldier* and it topped the Burgerville bestseller list three years in a row—an accomplishment Simon is proud to point out paid for his braces.

That's probably why Simon can be excited about senior year. Why he can miss Jane and still talk about buying shoes. In the world of the Blackburns, misfortune is just an inevitable stumbling block on the road to fame and fortune.

For some people, though, the past is too heavy; you can only move so far until you start to sink.

Or, since Rich is always correcting my use of second person: I can only move so far until I start to sink.

253 DAYS BEFORE

ALTERNATIVE DIMENSIONS

The first time I actually spoke to Jane was during class the day after she made her grand entrance. Mr. Parker was out sick, which wasn't a surprise, considering his illnesses usually coincided with various comic book conventions. He'd lined up Mr. Coots as a substitute, a man who had perfected the art of taking naps in public places, with schools being his specialty. Coots lost his pinky finger in the Vietnam War and typically spoke as if he were yelling over a helicopter. He always appeared on edge, like he expected the class to rebel and take over. He would read the newspaper and eventually fall asleep, at which point the class would descend into chaos until the bell rang. Sometimes he'd wake up, look disoriented, as if still caught in a dream, then share the story about how he lost his finger. "You know what I was doing when I was your age?!" he'd bark at the class. Everyone would stop what they were doing and listen.

"I was in 'Nam!" he'd yell.

Blank stares.

"Vietnam!" he'd yell again. "Fighting the North Vietnamese Army! That's how I lost this!"

He'd hold up the stub of his finger and make a biting motion. "Damn NVA soldier bit 'er right off!"

Someone would work up the courage to ask him what happened to the soldier, and the story was different every time.

The gratuitous: "I bit off his finger and cooked it in a stew!"

The inexplicable: "We're good friends now!"

The simple: "He's dead!"

The mind-fuck: "There *was* no NVA soldier!"

On this particular day, he was still asleep, reclining far back in his chair, eyes closed, lightly snoring. Spitballs littered his desk, the result of a five-dollar bounty for the first person able to hit him right between the eyes.

I finished the worksheet—a comic strip of RNA rescuing DNA—and proceeded to zone out, imagining ways I could find an excuse to talk to the mysterious stranger who now sat next to me. Every so often, I'd glance at her, pretending to look at the clock. It made me feel daring, like I was stealing fire from the gods.

She had on a huge pair of headphones that looked like earmuffs. Instead of doing the worksheet, she was drawing something in her notebook. She tapped her foot on the floor in a double-time rhythm, the nervous patter syncing up with the faint sound of acoustic guitar escaping her headphones.

Then a miracle happened. She took off her headphones and placed a folded piece of paper on my desk. I opened it with the awe of a pirate receiving a treasure map. On it, there was a drawing of Coots peacefully napping at his desk, drool spilling out of his mouth, hair coming out of his ears, while outside the window what looked to be a nuclear explosion billowed into a mushroom cloud. On the bottom, Jane had written: *Trade you this fine piece of art for the answers?*

I laughed and turned to look at her. She pointed at the worksheet, where Captain RNA and DNA Man were rambling on about mitochondria and alleles and all of their heroic exploits in the human body.

I couldn't think of anything to say, so I nodded and handed her the worksheet. She looked almost disappointed as she took the paper and began copying down the answers, like she was waiting for me to say something.

With girls in Burgerville, I'd always operated under the assumption that the less I spoke, the better. When I got nervous, I tended to tell really long and depressing stories about history. (*What? You don't want to hear about another brutal form of torture from the Middle Ages?*)

But not Jane. She seemed like one girl who might actually be interested in learning about the Head Crusher or Pear of Anguish.

It reminded me of this documentary I'd recently watched called *Alternative Dimensions*. They had a bunch of scientists and people in bow ties talking about how there are a million different universes out there with people just like us, only slightly different. After it ended, I had this sneaking suspicion that I was born in one of the bad dimensions—not nearly as bad as the one with giant insects, but still, not my first choice either. But when Jane entered the picture, it was like I suddenly found myself in the right dimension.

That day in class, I decided that no matter what, I had to talk to her. Even if I could only grunt or make high-pitched squeals, I'd force sound to vibrate off my vocal cords. I owed it to the Ray in one of the other dimensions who was out sick that day for eating an expired pudding the night before.

The clock ticked, her pencil moved furiously across the paper, and just when she was nearing the end of the worksheet, ready to scroll through her music and shut me out in a wall of sound, I asked the most idiotic question possible, muttered to new kids thousands of times every year, but still, at least it was English. "How do you like Burgerville so far?" The words stumbled over one another, vowels and consonants mixing into a gloppy soup.

She stopped writing and handed me the paper.

"I don't like it," she said.

"Me neither." I would've agreed with anything she'd said right then.

Instead of saying something more—that would have been the normal thing to do—I reverted to my usual tactic with girls, a staring contest that only *I* knew about. It's not like I didn't have any questions to ask her, it's just that none of them were related to anything going on in the moment. Like her favorite flavor of ice cream (strawberry, as I found out), her favorite book (*The Bell Jar*), whether she liked the *Star Wars* prequels (oddly enough, yes), the type of animal she'd most want to be ("A hedgehog, but a badass hedgehog, the kind that would attack you if you ever tried to put a hat on me").

"You know, Burgerville's actually not all bad," I found myself saying, almost as a reflex, a way to fill the empty space. And then a thought came to me as I scrolled through the history of Burgerville. "You said you liked conspiracy theories, right?"

Her eyes narrowed.

"Burgerville is home to one of the biggest conspiracies in the country. And no one outside of this town even knows about it."

I could tell Jane thought I was lying, but instead of calling me out or putting her headphones back on, she simply paused to think.

By then Mr. Coots had woken up. He looked around the room,

confused, on high alert for any signs of a communist sleeper cell. The class had stopped pretending to work and was involved in various forms of guerilla warfare against the system: Some kids were paying a boy named Peter Simmons to eat a moldy sandwich found in an abandoned lunchbox; others were recording videos of Coots to upload to the Facebook page entitled "Nap Time with Coots"; one kid was taking items out of Coots's bag and hiding them in various places around the room, a sort of cruel scavenger hunt for the elderly.

Coots rubbed his eyes. "What's going on in here?! Do you know what I was doing when I was your age?!"

After Coots finished telling us the story about his finger again, this one including an interesting twist about the NVA soldier immigrating to America and marrying Coots's sister, Jane turned to me and said, "Who are you?"

The way she said it I couldn't tell if she meant my name or what made me tick, the person underneath the labels.

"Raymond Green," I said, and put out my hand to shake.

She stared at my hand, then placed hers in mine.

"Pleased to meet you, Raymond Green," she said in a somewhat mocking tone. "I'm Jane Doe. So, are there a lot of weird places in this town?"

"Oh yeah, Burgerville's history will make you rethink everything you know about the past. And reality, for that matter."

Then, as my bravery began to leave me and I considered retreating, she said the most magical thing I'd ever heard: "Maybe you can show me?"

The universe collapsed and I found myself in a place I knew very little about: the dimension where good things happened.

98 DAYS AFTER

THE CIVIL RIGHTS FITNESS MOVEMENT OF RICHARD DAWSON

Twice a week I go to see Rich. When I first started seeing him, I looked him up on the internet to learn about his history, this guy who I'm supposed to be sharing all of my deepest, darkest secrets with. It turns out Rich was named after his grandfather Richard Dawson, a famous civil rights leader in the neighboring city of Centerville.

Richard Dawson started his career as a weight loss guru in the early 1950s, pioneering an exercise regimen built around everyday household activities. According to him, everything was an opportunity for getting in shape: chopping vegetables, turning doorknobs, vacuuming, mowing the lawn, even chewing, if done properly. At first people laughed at him, but when his clients began to see dramatic results, he landed a TV show on Burgerville County Public Access Television and became the first black television host in America.

During the Civil Rights Movement, he took his skills as a fitness motivator into the realm of race relations. He held marches like "Ten Miles for Equality" and organized a "Thirty-Day Challenge" where each day he urged people to do one thing to lessen racial inequality. His message was the same as his advice in fitness: Small steps matter, which is why he was such a big believer in marches and bus boycotts (though he disagreed with sit-ins for obvious reasons). And the cool thing is, even though some people criticized his simple approach, his strategies actually started to work. Centerville became the most integrated city in America. (And the fittest too.)

Sometimes it feels like Rich's therapy techniques come directly from his grandfather's playbook.

"Each day, I want you to do one thing that brings you and your mom closer," he said at our last session.

I rolled my eyes. I was sitting with my back to him at the time, in this big green leather rocking chair he must have bought at a tag sale. Pretty much everything in his office is old, which is probably why it smells like a cross between a gym locker and an old-age home. Faded motivational posters line the walls, a collection of cliché messages like *Every Journey Begins with a Single Step* and *You are the Creator of Your Own Destiny.*

"You mean like 'Ten Days to Be a Better Son'?" I asked.

"However many days it takes," Rich said.

I turned around to face him. I expected to see him playing a game on his cellphone, but instead he was staring straight ahead, a yellow notebook in his lap covered in writing.

"People are worried about you, Ray."

"I know."

"Should they be?"

"I don't know," I said.

Rich leaned forward; an alarm had been set off.

"I'm not gonna kill myself, if that's what you're thinking."

"Have you had thoughts about it?"

I sighed. "No. I didn't mean people should worry about *that*. I just meant in general. Like will I pass math and that sort of thing."

"How can I trust that you're telling me the truth?"

I'd never seen Rich so serious before.

"Relax," I said. "Jeez. You know I'd never do that."

He kept looking at me.

"I'll call you if anything changes, okay?"

"Day or night. And if not me, then your mom, your dad, Simon, *anyone*." He rummaged through his bag and handed me a pamphlet with a bunch of phone numbers and facts about suicide.

I folded it up and put it in my pocket. I just wanted the conversation to end.

"Now let's brainstorm some strategies to help you and your mom get along better," Rich said.

"How much time is left?" I asked. I could tell that kind of annoyed Rich, because he sat back and let his notepad fall to the floor.

"I can't do all the work," he said.

"But you're the only one getting paid," I said.

252 DAYS BEFORE

GREEN COW ACRES

Amidst the chaos that ensued after Coots fell back asleep on that fateful day in class—spitballs flying, lunchmeat being thrown, people taking cover under desks—Jane and I set up our "date." The plan was to meet at six o'clock in front of Earl Beddington's statue, the man at the center of the conspiracy. After I told her about Beddington and the legend of the green cows, I'd bring her to the place where it all started: the vacant lot known as Green Cow Acres.

Back in the 1950s, while the rest of America was wrapped up in Roswell hysteria, Burgerville experienced its own encounter with an alien species. One of the farmers went out of business during the Great Depression and his farm sat empty all throughout World War II. By the time the war ended, the land was overgrown and the animals that weren't sold had escaped into the surrounding countryside. Rumor spread that the escaped cows had turned a shade of green to blend in with their environment. Worse, many of the farmers believed the cows had become carnivores and were feeding on their genetic cousins. Strange sounds were reported, something between a cow's moo and a wolf's howl.

Soon an angry mob of townspeople formed—think pitchforks,

straw hats, and chants about killing mutant cows. Led by Earl Beddington, the town's most prominent farmer, the mob marched on the vacant field as soon as the sun went down. But the grass was so high and the farm so big, they eventually got lost in all the foliage. As midnight approached, they set up camp in a small clearing inside the jungle of grass. While the others slept, Beddington stood guard, his pitchfork grasped tightly in his hands.

A little before dawn, Beddington heard a rustling in the grass. He was about to go back to camp to warn the others when he came face-to-face with, you guessed it, a green cow.

But this wasn't just any ordinary cow with a green tint. According to Beddington, it had long fangs, pointed ears, and bright red eyes. The cow sniffed him the same way dogs do when you first meet them. Beddington said it made him feel like a piece of meat.

Beddington began to slowly back away. The beast licked its chops and then charged, all the while viciously mooing. Panicked, Beddington let out a high-pitched squeal and ran full sprint back toward the camp.

"Cows!" he yelled. "Cows!"

The rest of the posse woke up, grabbed their pitchforks, and ran as fast as they could. By the time the sun came up, three people had been impaled, one eye had been poked out, and Beddington was forever changed. A search party found the injured and frightened farmers soon after, their screams having carried throughout the town.

Beddington harbored revenge against cows for the rest of his life. He became an outspoken critic of vegetarianism, and much to the embarrassment of his family, an advocate of a theory he called spontaneous evolution.

Green Cow Acres was bulldozed a few years later. By then, the town had a new mayor, a new name—Williamsburg—and was trying to change its image from a backwater town to a real center for business and vacation homes. And that meant declaring the green cows weren't real and that Beddington was basically a crackpot.

But here's the conspiracy part: When they cleared the land, the rumor is they found the skull of a cow with incisors as big as steak knives. The mayor had the skull destroyed, but one of the construction workers sold the story to the press, and so the legend of the green cows lives on. Eventually, the town dedicated a statue to Beddington, honoring him for his role in developing Burgerville, but most people still know him as the guy who came face-to-face with a green cow and lived to tell the tale.

I arrived at Beddington's statue promptly at 5:45. Located in front of Town Hall, it's probably Burgerville's most famous landmark. I waited expectantly, an anxious feeling in the pit of my stomach, shivering on the unusually cold fall day. Beddington stared at the horizon in the direction of Green Cow Acres, a panicked expression on his marble face. His arms were opened, palms to the sky, still warning his fellow townsfolk about the green cows.

As the minutes passed, my hope began to wane. After about half an hour of nervously pacing, I went to face Beddington and find solace in his stone eyes. I nodded to him, thinking how foolish I was to think Jane actually liked me. Beddington seemed to be looking over my shoulder, keeping an eye out for his green cows.

After a while, I got the feeling he was looking at someone. I turned around, and there was Jane, her head tilted up at the statue. I almost jumped in surprise. Jane had her hands tucked in the pockets of a black hoodie, zipped all the way to her neck; her eyes reflected the last few rays of sunlight, two orbs glowing in the dusk. She peeled back her hood, revealing her long black hair, and once again my heart began to race as she walked closer.

"What's he looking for?" Jane asked, glancing over her shoulder in the direction of Green Cow Acres.

"You came," I said.

Jane surveyed the scene, turning around to take in the full scope of Burgerville's main drag. The dilapidated exterior of Town Hall, an oblong structure that resembled a prison, loomed over Beddington. A single traffic light blinked yellow, a recent addition that was part of the town council's push to modernize Burgerville.

"So this is it?" she asked.

The way she said it, I couldn't tell if she was talking about the statue or the town.

"Pretty much," I said, my words garbled. I had once again lost the ability to speak.

Jane hesitantly walked over to Beddington, leaned over, and read the inscription on the base of the statue.

"*Earl Beddington. Visionaries don't see with their eyes, they see with their hearts.*" Jane paused to ponder Beddington's words. "So, is this like your grandpa or something?"

I shook my head. "I wish. His relatives are loaded." I then proceeded to tell her about the green cows, Beddington's ill-fated search party, and the eventual cover-up. When I finished, Jane shook her head in disbelief.

"So you're saying that this guy believed the cows over there"— Jane turned and pointed toward Green Cow Acres—"had mutated and become carnivores?"

"That's right."

"And you guys built him a statue?"

"Not for the cows. For his other achievements."

"And no one talks about the green cows?"

"That's *all* people talk about."

"One delusional episode and no one can give the poor guy a break."

"Who knows," I said. "Maybe we're the delusional ones."

Jane climbed onto the base of the statue and cozied up to Beddington. His imposing figure dwarfed her slight frame.

"Take a picture," she said, reaching down to hand me her cellphone.

I snapped a photo, Jane giving a thumbs-up to the camera like she was posing with a minor celebrity.

"My friends will get a kick out of this," she said.

Jane teetered on the edge of the base, her arms spread out for balance.

"So why'd your family move to Burgerville?" I asked.

She jumped down from the statue, took her phone, and sat on the ground with her back to Beddington. "I'm still trying to figure that out myself," she said. She let her head fall back against the pedestal, a few inches in front of Beddington's boot. "Did you grow up here?"

I nodded.

"I'm sorry," she said, as if I'd just told her I had some horrible terminal illness.

Jane patted the ground next to her, inviting me to sit. I carefully lowered myself beside her and sat down cross-legged.

"My parents can't stop talking about all the fresh air," she said. "How quiet it is. All the wide-open spaces. When the nicest thing you can say about a place is that there isn't much there, I don't think that's a good thing."

"There's a lot of stuff here," I said, "you just can't see it all."

"Like green cows?"

"I don't know. I guess I mean the history."

"Please don't tell me you're one of those people who reenacts Civil War battles."

"No," I said, leaving out the time my grandfather took me to Burgerville's Civil War Remembrance Festival and we reenacted the Day of the Substitutes, a proud moment where the landowners of Burgerville paid people to fight for the Union. "I'm talking about the stories."

"You know they have those today too, right?"

"Yeah, but they're all so . . ." I struggled for the right words. "True."

We sat in silence, our shoulders lightly touching.

"So this guy Beddington," Jane said as the sun continued to dip below the horizon, "did he ever change his mind about the green cows?"

"Never. His family tried to quiet him down, but even on his deathbed, he told anyone who would listen about what he saw that day."

"Poor guy," Jane said. "It's kind of sad."

"Until the day someone spots another green cow. Then the story changes and the past is rewritten. That's why I like history so much."

"But it doesn't really change the past."

"No, but it changes how we see the past. Which is just as important."

"Unless you're Beddington," Jane said.

I felt Jane lean into my shoulder, her weight shifting almost imperceptibly. I let myself fall into her, careful not to breathe, worried the moment was too fragile.

"There's always room for revisions in history," I said.

"How about in life?"

Before I could respond, Jane stood up, brushed off her pants, and turned to face Beddington. She seemed to be looking for clues in his stoic expression. Grabbing Beddington's boot for leverage, I lifted myself off the ground and stood in front of Jane.

Just when I had worked up the courage to look into her eyes, I heard her phone beep. She pulled it out of her pocket, typed something, then said, "My ride's here. Thanks for the history lesson, Ray." She saluted Beddington and walked away.

"Where are you going?" I called after her.

"One of my friends from the city is picking me up," she said. As she scanned the street, glancing down at her phone every few seconds, a car approached, the headlights so bright, I had to look away.

"But don't you want to see Green Cow Acres?"

"I think I'll take a pass," she said, facing the street. "That place screams *dead bodies*."

I realized I had just been used. Clearly her main objective was meeting her friends from the city, but why go through all the trouble of meeting me at Beddington's statue? I could only guess that her parents were trying to keep her from her old life and I had been an alibi, a red herring meant to throw them off her trail.

An expensive-looking car with tinted windows pulled up. When Jane opened the back door, smoke billowed out.

The sun had all but gone down, so I couldn't really make out the person in the driver's seat. I heard laughter, a loud bass trembling in the trunk, and a voice asking if the statue of Beddington was Abraham Lincoln. I cringed. Jane, realizing the ridiculousness of her friend's comment, rolled her eyes and shrugged her shoulders. Then, just as I was about to turn around and head home, she called out to me.

"Ray," she said, her voice barely audible over the music.

"Yeah?"

"I hope you find your green cows."

I nodded, standing in the middle of Beddington's growing shadow. "You too."

Jane dipped into the car and slammed the door. As I watched the taillights recede in the distance, I wondered whether or not I had just had my own encounter with something not really there. I normally would have brushed off the thought, but after that night, Jane seemed to disappear.

She wasn't in school the next day, the day after that, and then the entire week. I was sure her parents had woken up, recognized they'd made a mistake, and moved somewhere else.

I settled into my routine of zoning out during class and lunch with Simon, where we'd discuss topics like the worst way to die and whether or not we'd cut off various body parts to date hot girls in our grade. Simon and I had no choice but to accept the Burgerville status quo. A place where girls ignored us, I was the weird kid who liked history, and Simon was the even weirder kid who wanted to be a vampire—or, according to one rumor started in middle school, *was* a vampire.

"You've got to forget about her," Simon told me at lunch after a full week of speculating about Jane's whereabouts, a long list that included North Dakota, North Korea, and the North Pole.

"I can't," I said.

"There are plenty of fish in the sea."

But we both knew that wasn't true. At least not in the dry, desolate lake of Burgerville.

"She's different," I said.

"What makes her so special? Besides the fact that she talked to you."

I had an image of her in my mind. Perpetually walking into Mr. Parker's classroom. That look of confusion, like she was trying to figure out where she was, *who* she was.

"I don't know," I said. "But that's the thing. I really want to find out."

"Maybe you scared her away," Simon said.

"Good talk," I said, throwing a french fry at Simon's face.

Once again, the best things about Burgerville remained in the past.

At least that's what I thought.

112 DAYS AFTER

LIGHT THERAPY

Rich has been giving me all these assignments lately to help me better understand myself and my depression. "Depression is like this black light on everything in your life so you can only see the bad stuff," he explains. "We're trying to give you a flashlight to help you see all the good stuff too."

"But don't black lights reveal the truth? I saw this special on hotels—"

"You're missing the point, Ray." He pauses, looks around the room. "Let me ask you this. Do historians only study the endings of events?"

"No," I say.

"And why's that?"

"Because history isn't a straight line from the beginning to the end. You've got to study everything in between. That's where the real answers are."

"And do they leave out all of the good parts? Is the story of Burgerville just a bunch of Beddingtons looking for green cows?"

"No. You have to have balance. Both the good and the bad. You have to tell the truth."

"Good. So maybe you have to become a better historian of yourself." He leans forward, a smug look on his face, as if he expects applause.

I roll my eyes. He sounds like . . . Well, he sounds kind of like me when I used to give Jane those same speeches.

"Is that clock wrong?" I ask. It feels like we've been talking for hours, but only about ten minutes have passed.

Rich glances at the clock. Instead of numbers, there are bright yellow faces representing moods—happiness, sadness, anger, one that looks like a homicidal maniac, which, according to its placement, is Rich's three o'clock.

"Look, Ray, getting better isn't about waking up with a big smile on your face and suddenly feeling like everything makes sense. It's about taking a lot of little steps."

I point to one of the posters on the wall. "We're back at the motivational posters?"

"They're clichés for a reason. So this week I want you to look at a few situations through the lens of a black light and a flashlight. I'm calling it 'Light Therapy.'"

"Catchy," I say.

So here it goes:

SITUATION ONE

Black Light: Simon spent all lunch talking about his new shoes, complaining that the lights had already grown dimmer from when he first opened the box. It was like our year with Jane never happened. When I didn't respond, he initiated a heart-to-heart, telling me to cheer up and try to get excited about senior year. "Life happens," he said, "whether you're awake for it or not. And given your sleeping condition, you should really try to live life to the fullest." I wanted to yell at him and ask, "What about Jane?"

Flashlight: Maybe Simon's just trying to be a good friend. I know he misses Jane too. A few times this school year he's begun telling a story about her and then stopped mid-sentence, his voice breaking, eyes on the verge of tears. At that point, he'll put away his Lunchable—yes, Simon still eats Lunchables—and say he has diarrhea or needs to go to the bathroom to apply his acne medication, something way more embarrassing than just admitting he's crying.

SITUATION TWO

Black Light: I drew the short straw and got Mr. Hillman, the worst teacher in the entire school, for U.S. Foreign Relations. Mr. Hillman resembles Napoleon in his later years, barely five five, with a receding hairline and sagging jowls that carve his face into a permanent frown. He also has all of the insecurities associated with the Napoleon Complex. Most of his lessons somehow circle back to one of his accomplishments. Already, U.S. Foreign Relations is feeling a lot like an extended introduction to Mr. Hillman's time as a track star in college.

Flashlight: Some history is better than no history.

SITUATION THREE

Black Light: My mom spent last Saturday cleaning out the garage, untouched since my dad left, filled with boxes of yellowed papers, clothes from when I was a kid, and the elephant in the room, all of my dad's old stuff. As weird as it is to say, something about being surrounded by all that stuff, all that history, was kind of comforting. So if I wanted to look at my clothes from childhood— priceless items like my old cowboy boots and neon-blue track suit—they were there. If I wanted to read my ambitious tome on the history of the french fry, written in fifth grade, I just had to find the right crate. And if I wanted to look at my dad's old yearbooks, pictures of his fraternity brothers, or his old baseball glove, all those things were there too—well, at least they were, until my mom crammed everything of his in a box labeled *Goodwill* and packed it in her trunk. It feels like she's erasing his memory, cutting out all the good parts of our history with the bad.

Flashlight: Just because I'm stuck in the past, doesn't mean my mom has to be too.

237 DAYS BEFORE

NEVER HAVE I EVER

About two weeks after our encounter at Beddington's statue, Jane showed up unexpectedly at my house, my own green cow come to life. Simon and I were in my room, watching a horror movie called *The Butcher* with the sound off and filling in the dialogue ourselves—a favorite pastime of ours, especially with movies that look like they're made on someone's cellphone.

In the movie, a group of four college students go to explore an abandoned meat factory. Don't ask me why; I think it has something to do with a sorority initiation gone wrong, but I don't think the writer was all that concerned with plot. Let's be honest: People watch the movie because of the interesting ways people are eaten by the Butcher.

When you watch so many of these low-budget horror movies, you start to see how all of the characters have a very specific role to fulfill, like they're all different parts of a recipe. But with the sound off you don't hear all the cheesy movie dialogue, so they just seem like good people caught in really bad situations.

Take the CWDF, or the Character Who Dies First. I always feel sympathy for them because they really only exist to move the story along. And who wants to think that their whole purpose in life is to create more suspense for everyone else?

The UBF, or Ugly Best Friend, doesn't have it easy either. How sad for them that their main role is to make the main character seem really good-looking and nice and likeable and all that. It really makes you wonder, can life be full of main characters? Or do some of us have to play supporting roles?

Even the TF, or Topless Female, is a hero in her own way. Movie after movie, these actresses help Hollywood producers increase ticket sales, bravely going shirtless in the cold, like they do in *Vampire Snowman* (Volumes 1–5), or spending hours chained up naked in some dingy basement, like they do in the extremely gory and violent *Dingy Basement*. Boobs really shouldn't be used as a way to get people to watch movies. I hardly ever pause those scenes anymore, and when I do, I feel pretty guilty about it.

Anyway, we were in the middle of a kill scene involving barbecue sauce and macaroni salad, the kind of gory spectacle that instead of scaring you makes you laugh at how ridiculous it is. Just as the Butcher was about to hang the CWDF on a meat hook, and Simon was filling in the Butcher's line with "I hate to leave you hanging," the doorbell rang.

Simon and I stared at each other.

I nodded to the TV. "Could it be the Butcher?"

"Come for the perfect cut of meat?"

"It's possible."

I heard my mom open the door. Muffled voices followed by the sound of the door closing. No struggle, no crazy laugh, no creepy line about a Filet Man-yon. Simon and I both sighed with relief.

My mom called up the stairs. "Ray, you have a visitor?" There was a slight rise in pitch at the end, like she couldn't believe it herself.

I pressed pause on the DVD, right on a shot of the Butcher preparing some sort of stew with an ear bobbing at the surface.

Simon looked at me strangely, as if he thought I'd been hiding friends from him.

I shrugged. "I have no idea."

I walked out of my room with a heaviness in my stomach. As I rounded the corner at the top of the stairs, I saw Jane and immediately stopped. Her black hair shielded her face, but the silhouette was unmistakable. She had been all I could think about for the past couple of weeks and now she stood in my living room.

A thought suddenly struck me: *She's making awkward small talk with my mom.* I thought of all the unfortunate comments my mom could make: *Ray doesn't get many visitors. Who put you up to this? We take bullying very seriously.*

I sprang out from behind the wall and ran down the stairs, almost slipping as I reached the bottom.

I must have startled Jane, because she jumped a little when I descended the final stair.

"Hi," I said, out of breath.

"Hi," she said.

She looked tired. Dark eye shadow and bags under her eyes. Her voice sounded hoarse.

My mom stood between us. I could feel her eyes on me, accusingly: *Have you just been pretending to be a nerd this entire time?*

"Do you want to offer your friend something to drink?" she asked.

I stared blankly at Jane and then attempted to ask, but the noise came out as a grunt.

Jane shook her head. "I'm okay, but thanks." The silence expanded. I repeatedly blinked, hoping it might snap me out of my caveman daze.

My mom's eyes darted back and forth from Jane to me. "I'll be in the kitchen," she said, and made her exit. Glancing back over her shoulder as she left, she had this weird look on her face, one eyebrow raised, like she couldn't quite piece together the puzzle.

Part of me wanted to run after her, grab her leg, and scream, "Take me with you!" Instead, the part of me still going through puberty kicked in; I lowered my voice and puffed out my chest. "What brings you here?" I asked.

"I wanted to say sorry for ditching you a couple of weeks ago." She scanned the room, lingering on the baby picture with my exceptionally large head, eyes darting past the off-color square on the wall where my parents' wedding portrait used to hang, all the way to the ceramic sculpture of a giraffe I made in fourth grade, perched on the mantel like a phallic-inspired deity.

"I tried to escape," Jane said after she finished her stationary tour of my living room.

We remained standing by the stairs. The light from the chandelier cast shadows around us. Our shadow selves stood on the edge, watching us.

"What happened?" I asked.

"They caught me," she said. "And now here I am."

She sighed, as if being in my house was one of the worst fates that could befall a person.

"Your mom said you're having a sleepover," she said. "So what are you guys doing?"

"On Fridays we watch horror movies."

"Cute." She motioned to the stairs. "Shall we?"

Together, we walked up the steps. We paused at the top, Jane waiting for direction. I pointed to the right and followed Jane down the hallway toward my bedroom.

Just as she reached the door, Simon opened it.

He rubbed his eyes the same way people do in movies when they're in the desert and see an oasis in the distance.

"This is Simon," I said.

"Sorry to bust up your play date, Simon."

Simon's mouth hung wide open.

"This is Jane," I said. No explanation necessary. I'd been talking to Simon about her ever since that first day I saw her in Mr. Parker's class.

She brushed by, barely giving Simon time to get out of her way.

Suddenly everything in my room became the worst thing imaginable. The action figures on my desk made me seem like a kindergartner. My only trophy, a monument to my miraculous win in the eighth-grade spelling bee, looked like a pathetic cry for help. The plate of cookies that my mom had "baked with love" now mocked Simon and me from the corner, two overgrown children watching scary movies on a Friday night.

Jane grabbed a cookie off the plate, took a bite, and sat down on my bed. "What are we watching?"

"*The Butcher,*" I said.

"Who's for dinner?" she said, repeating the movie's tagline.

"Where have you been?" I asked.

"New York."

"You just decided to leave?"

"Yeah, no offense, but I don't know how you guys take it. I feel like I'm in a hundred years ago."

"That's part of the fun," Simon said. He then remembered himself and lowered his gaze to the ground.

"It's just so much nothing," Jane said. "Unless you're talking about green cows."

She winked at me. But all exaggerated, like she was . . . Oh my god, was she flirting with me?

"You mean you've seen one?" Simon asked.

Jane laughed. "No. But even if I did, I wouldn't tell anyone."

"But you could end up with your own statue," I said.

"Or in a mental institution."

"Or both," Simon said.

Simon pressed play on the movie and raised the volume. "Tastes like chicken," the Butcher said to his unfortunate date. "I thought it *was* chicken," his date said. We all gasped in horror as the Butcher opened a fridge with the CWDF's head in it, his face frozen in anguish.

Jane brought her hands to her eyes so she wouldn't have to see the TV. Blood-curdling screams echoed in the background.

"I hate horror movies," she said.

"It's a true story," Simon said, staring at the screen.

"Even worse."

Her reaction surprised me. For some reason—chalk it up to the heavy black boots and dark eye shadow—I'd assumed she would love blood and gore.

Simon turned the TV off. "It's only fun for the dinner scenes."

"I have Jenga," I said.

Jane began to pick fuzz off her sweatshirt, a black hoodie with a picture of what looked to be a possum with wings. *The Flying Possum of Williamsburg* was written beneath the picture in bright red. Yet another obscure reference to her old life?

"Jenga never disappoints," Simon said.

But Jane had already decided against it. "Have you guys ever played Never Have I Ever?"

Simon and I stared at her blankly.

"It's really simple. Basically, someone says something they've never done . . . and if it's something you've done yourself, you drink." Jane started rummaging through her bag. "But I play it a little differently. It doesn't make sense that the people with the most experience end up drinking the most. So, in my rules, you drink only when you *haven't* done something."

"Drink what?" Simon asked innocently.

She pulled a small bottle from her bag. "Just a sip. Unless you guys want to play with milk to go along with those," she said, pointing to the cookies. Simon, not getting the joke, nodded his head and raced downstairs to retrieve some milk.

Jane studied my room while we waited.

"I feel like I've seen this room on a sitcom."

"Thanks."

"You're welcome," she said. "I guess." She raised her eyebrows and looked around. The air became thick with silence, and I wished real life had a laugh track or canned *awws* to take away the awkwardness.

Simon burst through the door carrying a gallon of milk. "Your mom told me she buys milk just for me," he said. "Do you think she's trying to tell me something?"

I rolled my eyes and shook my head, as if to say, *Not now, we have a guest.*

"I'll start," Jane said. "Never have I ever gone cow tipping."

"People don't actually go cow tipping," I said.

Simon had a guilty look on his face. "It was only once, I swear."

"Bottoms up," she said as she passed me the bottle. I took a sip and my throat practically burst into flames. I wanted to gag, spit it out, take an action figure, and go hide in the corner.

"First drink?" she asked.

"Today," I said. Jane gave me a quizzical look. She could see right through me.

"It was with my uncle," Simon said apologetically, still on the cows. "It was the worst thing I've ever done." He took a sip of his milk, ignoring the rules of the game. He wiped his milk mustache and took a bite out of a cookie.

"Your turn," Jane said to Simon.

"Never have I ever done drugs," Simon said proudly. It sounded like a PSA for kids.

I took another sip. I had never even seen drugs.

Jane laughed and took the bottle from me. She pretended to bring it to her lips, then quickly put it down. "I thought living here would make anyone do drugs." She turned to me. "Have you thought of one, Ray?"

I collected my thoughts. "Never have I ever wet the bed."

This time Jane took a big sip of the syrupy liquid.

Simon remained staring at his milk, caught in a battle of his conscience versus his thirst. He put his milk down and dropped his head in his hands. "What?" he said. "Everyone has their demons."

Jane patted Simon on the shoulder and nodded at me to do the same.

As we both comforted Simon, Jane smiled at me. And in that brief moment, time stretched out and I realized I'd been waiting for that look my entire life. Hoping for it. And I didn't know it until right then.

After a few seconds, Simon picked his head up. "You won't tell anyone, right?"

"Friends don't tell each other's secrets. Right, Ray?"

"Consider it off the historical record," I said.

"Wait, did you say 'friend' before?" Simon asked.

"You're up," I said to Jane, not wanting her to clarify. A sinister smile formed at the edge of her lips. "Never have I ever kissed a girl," she said.

Simon and I looked at each other. We both knew the truth. The only question was whether or not we'd admit it in front of Jane. The age-old battle of ethics versus survival. I saw Simon bring the milk up to his lips and imagined diving out in front of him to slap the bottle away.

Instead, I grabbed the alcohol and drank along with him. I took an extra-big sip, bravely facing my fate.

We both slowly pulled the bottles away from our mouths. Simon wiped his milk mustache on his sleeve as I coughed into mine.

"Really?" she asked after we'd finished. "Never?"

We both shook our heads.

She shrugged, but that was it. She didn't laugh or call us losers or anything like that. Instead, she pointed at Simon and told him it was his turn. Once again, I got the feeling we were in an alternative universe, one where the popular kids sat alone at lunch, had their houses egged, and were slammed into lockers. And in that dimension, I was captain of the football team and Simon was prom king.

We kept playing for another hour or so, though Simon and I did most of the drinking. My head was spinning by the time Jane stashed what was left of the small bottle of alcohol in her purse, walked over to my window, and said she had to leave.

"You can go through my front door," I said, slurring my speech.

She opened the window and reached out to touch the old tree that grew right next to my room.

"I'm fulfilling a lifelong dream," she said. "Some things you just can't do in the city." I watched as she climbed out of the window and placed both feet on the branch until only her head and torso were visible over the edge. Simon shyly waved good-bye and held his stomach with his free hand. He let out a loud burp.

"You sure you're okay?" I asked her. I forced myself to make eye contact. Her eyes were practically closed, but instead of making her seem more distant, she appeared softer and less guarded.

"It's a lot scarier on a sixth-floor walk-up," she said. She motioned for me to come closer, half of her body still hanging out the window. I walked over to her. "So where are you taking me next?" she asked.

I had to lean in to make sure I heard her correctly.

"It depends," I said. "What do you want to see?"

"Something that makes me question whether or not we're actually living in someone's bizarre dream. Or nightmare."

"That's easy."

Our faces were only inches apart. She leaned closer to me. I could smell the alcohol on her breath.

The whole scene was apparently too much for Simon. His stomach gurgled, a bubble that made its way up to his throat in a volcano of milk and cookie. He spewed all over my carpet. By the time I had a chance to turn back, Jane had already left.

234-228 DAYS BEFORE

THE HISTORY OF BURGERVILLE

After our Never Have I Ever game, I made a list of a few places in Burgerville Jane and I could visit. I scoured my history books, looking for all of the weirdest stories, the legends, the ones that lay somewhere between reality and *God, I hope that's not true*.

I showed Jane the list in biology first thing on Monday morning. Mr. Parker was trying a new tactic in class. Instead of making us read his made-up comics about biology, he'd created an assignment based on finding the science in *Batman* and *Superman*.

"Now listen, class," Mr. Parker said. "You might be saying to yourself, what relevance do the Metropolis Marvel and the Caped Crusader have to our study of biology?" He paused, handed out some dog-eared comics, then quickly retreated behind his computer. He either forgot to finish his thought or didn't really have an answer himself.

While Mr. Parker browsed a used comic books website—he forgot to take his computer off the projector—Jane and I read through the list.

The History of Burgerville
 1) Town Hall

2) The Lost Woods

3) The McCallen Mansion

4) The Burgerville Annual Spring Festival

5) Green Cow Acres

"Burgerville's Grand Tour," I said after we talked through the list. "A walk through the bizarre history of the most interesting town in America."

Jane raised an eyebrow.

"I'm not talking about now. I'm talking about then."

"Fair enough," she said. "And I see you saved Green Cow Acres for last?"

"I'm hoping that by then you'll know I'm not a serial killer."

"That line sounds like it was lifted directly out of the serial killer handbook."

"So you've read the handbook?"

"You got me there," Jane said. "What's life without taking a few chances, anyway?"

"Exactly," I said. I looked at her T-shirt. An alien ominously peered over an operating table. *Area 52* was scrawled across the top above the caption: *And you thought Area 51 was bad . . .*

Jane looked down. "Pretty scary, huh? My best friend, Ellie, gave it to me. She's the one who got me into conspiracy theories."

"He looks familiar," I said, pointing at the lanky alien.

"You mean you've met . . ." At which point, Jane made a loud noise, something that sounded like a velociraptor giving birth. Everyone in the class turned to look.

"I'm actually thinking of his cousin Pete," I said. "Kind of like"—I attempted to make the same noise—"but with a goatee."

She slapped me on the shoulder. "You're funny."

For some reason, Jane had chosen me as her Burgerville emissary. I felt everyone in class watching as Jane and I talked. At one point, Jane leaned in to draw a picture of the two of us journeying through history on what looked to be a pterodactyl. I smelled her hair in a completely non-creepy way and our arms touched. That, coupled with our shoulder touch at Beddington's statue, had been the most female contact I'd had since Mrs. Romano hugged me before summer vacation the previous school year. I imagined everyone in class holding their breath.

Raymond Green, the dork who loved history, hanging out with the mysterious new girl. Not even the best historian could have seen that coming.

The Burgerville rumor mill had been speculating about Jane ever since her first appearance in school. She didn't fit the Burgerville mold, but that only made her cooler.

"Her parents are in witness protection," one source said.

"She's going to be my best friend," a popular girl said. "My parents are gonna hate it."

Jocks like Tommy Beddington, the resident football star of Burgerville and grandson of the late Earl Beddington, had reportedly already called dibs on her, as if dating in high school was as easy as calling shotgun.

"Beddington," Simon said, balling his hand into a fist when I brought him up at lunch.

"You've got to let it go," I said.

Simon and I had never really fit in, but it wasn't until freshman year that people really started bullying us. That year, Beddington smeared chocolate pudding on Simon's chair—right before he had to introduce his grandfather the Korean War antihero to the entire school. The principal had gotten involved and made Beddington promise to leave us alone. After that, we'd been even more aggressively ignored.

But Simon still hadn't forgiven Beddington for what we'd come to call "Puddinggate."

"I'll let it go when the debt has been repaid," Simon said, taking a sip out of his carton of milk. Not the ones sold in the cafeteria, but a half-gallon his mom packed in his lunch every day. He wiped his milk mustache.

"You're scaring me," I said.

"Thanks," he said.

The rumors didn't stop with Jane. Simon and I also found ourselves the subject of discussion around school, as people speculated why the new girl was hanging out with *us*. We were just as confused as everyone else. I remember this miraculous moment when the tables parted and Jane threw her stuff down on our lunch table and sarcastically asked, "Is this seat taken?" To which Simon gulped and replied, "Sometimes the lunch ladies eat with us."

Some kids assumed we were blackmailing Jane, or at least paying her to elevate our social status.

Jennifer Robinson was less kind and also embarrassingly misinformed about world history: "They ordered her online from the Soviet Union."

Others thought our odd group must be some sort of social experiment: "It's like one of those anti-bullying campaigns," said an undisclosed source.

"Maybe she's after our money," Simon said.

"What money?"

Simon shrugged, as if he hadn't thought of that before.

"Maybe she just likes us," I said.

"Be serious, Ray."

Before Jane, we'd existed in a world of our own, an empty lunch table where we'd trade stories about history all the while dreaming of the future—a time when girls paid attention to us and, in Simon's case, the mullet came back in style. But Jane completely flipped the script.

The story of Burgerville had changed.

125 DAYS AFTER

JENGA

I've been telling Rich a lot about those first few weeks—meeting Jane, the way she made me feel, how for the first time in my life I actually cared about the *now*. Rich always smiles and waits patiently, then says something like, "She'll always be an important part of your life, and it's important to remember that as we take some little steps forward." Then he'll suggest one of his challenges, maybe "Three Things You're Thankful For," or one of my favorites, "Two Weeks to Make a New Friend."

At our last session, I got so tired of hearing all his clichés that I kind of snapped at him.

"Do you and my mom have the same book of motivational phrases?" I asked, my voice slightly raised.

He looked surprised by my sudden outburst of emotion.

I collected myself. "It's not like I can just choose which parts to remember and which parts to forget."

He nodded, waiting for me to continue.

"It's like a game of Jenga," I told him. "I don't know which pieces I can take out. If you take out the wrong piece, it all comes crashing down."

I was pretty proud of my metaphor, so I let it breathe, let Rich soak it in.

"I've never heard a better metaphor about Jenga," Rich said. "But what happens when everything comes crashing down?"

"You start over."

"So if you never try, you're just stuck playing the same game."

"Yes, but . . ."

I guess it wasn't as good of a metaphor as I thought, because I could tell Rich had already found the loophole.

"Maybe I should have chosen a different game," I said, "because you're missing the point."

"Which is?"

"I don't want to start another game. *That's* the point."

"Sometimes you don't have a choice."

I'm not one of those people who becomes a puddle of emotions at the drop of a hat. I don't cry during movies, pictures of puppies don't warm my heart, and I've never written a poem about the sadness of the moon. But something about this conversation bothered me. It felt like a lie.

"Are we done yet?"

"We still have—"

But I was already on my way out the door. "I'll see you next week," I mumbled.

People, especially adults, just give up. If something goes wrong, they move on. Get over it. Stop looking in the rearview mirror.

I think they're just lazy.

222 DAYS BEFORE

TOWN HALL

The Friday after our Never Have I Ever game, we decided to head to Town Hall, the first spot on the list.

Simon agreed to pick Jane and me up, which meant he'd be driving his mom's brand-new red minivan. "Watch this," he said proudly in my driveway as he opened the sliding doors with the click of a button.

"That would have been much more impressive if this wasn't a minivan," I said.

Simon clicked another button. "For that, you've lost window privileges."

We drove on to meet Jane at her house. She gave us only a street name, which happened to be all the way on the opposite end of Burgerville. We were instructed to text her once we found her street.

"You sure this is a good spot for our first date?" Simon asked on the way over. "I mean, don't get me wrong, it makes one hell of a field trip, but maybe we should start with coffee first."

"*We're* not going on a date, Simon. I don't even think *I'm* going on a date."

"And you're positive this isn't just a ruse for the popular kids to throw eggs and toilet paper at us?"

"Jane wouldn't do that," I said. "She's like us."

"Do you know us?"

Simon pressed a button and the top of the car peeled back, revealing a gigantic moon roof with a panoramic view of the sky. "It's sort of like a convertible," Simon said.

"Exactly like a convertible," I said, hoping to win back my right to roll down the window.

As we drove, the houses gradually got bigger and farther apart. By the time we reached Jane's street, we were in a part of Burgerville I'd only read about: the New York Strip, so named because it was a vacation destination for many city dwellers. The houses sat on the edge of the Lost Woods, a gigantic nature preserve, and cost millions of dollars. Those who lived in the core of Burgerville—in the Marrow, if you will—could only hope to be invited over by one of their wealthy acquaintances to see what life was like for Burgerville's elite.

"I've never been this far before," Simon said.

"It's too late to turn back now," I said.

Simon unlocked my window.

"It's been an honor to have you as my copilot." He glanced at me uncertainly, then slowed to a crawl, trees on either side of us obscuring the castle-like mansions.

"We don't belong here," he said.

"This is our town," I replied.

"No, this is their town, we just live in it." Simon stopped the car. "Text her," he said.

As soon as I took out my phone, we heard a knock from the back. Simon and I both jumped.

"Open up, *Dad*," we heard muffled through the door.

Simon pressed a button and the minivan doors opened like an alien spaceship.

"That's the coolest thing I've ever seen," Jane said, hopping in the back.

Simon gave me a satisfied look before closing the doors and launching toward our final destination.

Burgerville's Town Hall looms over Earl Beddington's statue. Designed by an architect named Edward P. Delaney, it showcases a style called Absurdist Imperfectionism, based on displaying the human condition through strange—and sometimes dangerous—designs.

There are the revolving doors that take you right back outside, the slightly different-sized steps, and my favorite, the door that opens to a four-story fall, only boarded up when Mayor Elmer Stanton plunged to his untimely death in the early eighties. Depending on who you talk to, Delaney was a mad genius or just a shitty architect whose designs were always a little off. I like to believe the former.

On the ceiling of the lobby there's a mural of Burgerville, depicting the entire history of the town from the Mohegan people who originally lived on the land all the way to the current mayor, a man by the name of Albert Tomkins who'd been elected on his promise to give a free fanny pack to every eligible voter—two if you found a way to vote twice. The mural was basically an alternate history that ignored the truth of Burgerville's past. According to the mural, Burgerville's elders had bought the land fair and square from the Mohegan people. Instead of hiring substitutes to fight for them in the Civil War, they'd bravely marched into battle. For the section on World War II, Burgerville's important manufacturing contributions were highlighted, while the mass conversion to Quakerism to avoid direct service was entirely missing.

The three of us stood inside the lobby, tracing the town's version of its history while I explained what actually happened.

"It's like they just made stuff up," Jane said after we'd gone through all the lies it included.

"Exactly. But it's just true enough to trick people. That's why Roger Lutz started a petition to have it changed."

"Who's Roger Lutz?"

"You don't know Roger Lutz? He's Burgerville's preeminent historian. Everyone knows Roger Lutz. Right, Simon?"

"The old guy who used to come to our classes? Didn't he do your birthday once?"

"That's him."

"Must have been some party," Jane said. "So I take it the petition wasn't successful?"

"He could only get about a hundred signatures. A little while later, he was diagnosed with Alzheimer's."

"That sucks," Jane said.

I shrugged. "He's still in the archives every day. He said that just because *his* past is disappearing, it doesn't mean he's gonna let that happen to Burgerville's."

We made eye contact. I tried not to look away, but there was something so weird about the moment, like I was living it and remembering it at the same time. I became aware of my blinking, my palms sweating, the need to swallow. Jane finally saved me by looking up at the ceiling.

"What's next?"

"The roof. That's where—"

Before I could finish my sentence, Jane was walking toward the stairwell, pulling me along. We collected Simon, who was taking a picture of a bench dedicated to his great-grandfather, and then made our way up the stairs.

The sun was just beginning to set when we opened the door to the roof. Burgerville spread out around us, the leaves beginning to change, trees shining in the fading sunlight. Jane walked toward the middle, stopping in front of a stone fountain that resembled a gigantic birdbath.

"What's this?" Jane asked.

"The reason we're here. The Edward P. Delaney Memorial Wishing Well. In honor of all the debt he'd left Burgerville in. His design had so many little flaws that the town needed to find a way to make renovations. So they started planting stories in the newspaper about wishes mysteriously coming true. People being cured of diseases, winning the lottery, getting promotions. Suddenly growing a few inches. After a while, people started coming from all over the place, making their pilgrimage to Town Hall."

"How much money could you make from a few coins?"

"It wasn't the coins," I said. "It was the ticket to get onto the roof. But I'm sure they used the loose change too."

"I can't tell if you're making this up," Jane said.

"It's all true," I said proudly.

I reached into my pocket, passed a coin to Simon, kept one for me, and gave a small handful to Jane, my primitive way to show her I liked her. Me give you lots of metal.

"What are you doing?" Jane asked, looking down at the pile of change in her hand.

"Giving you wishes," I said.

Jane rolled her eyes. But smiled a little too.

Simon stood over the fountain. "I'm debating between ending world hunger and a trampoline," he said, then threw the coin in.

"What'd you decide?" Jane asked.

"I can't tell you that. Otherwise it might not come true."

I threw my coin into the fountain from a few feet away. I wished for things to actually work out for once. For Jane to like me. For her to be my girlfriend.

Jane was next. She stood over the water, eyes moving from me to Simon and back again, before letting the change slip out of her hand.

"The problem with wishes," she said, "is that no one ever tells you what they wished for. So you never know if it came true."

"You're saying it'd be nice to have some data on the effectiveness of wishing wells?"

"That's exactly what I'm saying," Jane said. She peered into the fountain. "I mean, look at all those wishes. People hoping to fall in love, get divorced, become dictator of their own private island."

I followed Jane's lead and stared down at the murky water, coins gleaming beneath the surface. "People wishing they could erase the past."

"Or change the past," Jane said.

"Or become a vampire."

Jane and I gave Simon a funny look.

"Let's make a deal," Jane said. "If any of our wishes come true, we have to tell each other about it." Simon and I agreed. We formed a circle and put our hands in the middle like a team getting ready for a game. I felt Jane's hand beneath mine. My heart started racing. We looked at one another, trying to figure out what the next step was, the proper way to seal a pact.

"Clearly none of us have ever played team sports," I said.

"Don't we throw our hands up in the air?" Simon asked, sounding unsure.

"I'm pretty sure there's some sort of pumping motion," Jane said.

"On three?"

As we kept discussing, the circle slowly disintegrated, until we all just agreed to a verbal pact.

"We're not huddle people," Jane said.

After that we walked to the edge of the roof and watched the sun go down on Burgerville, and I felt Jane's hand brush against mine. Then miraculously, our fingers clasped. I took a deep breath so I wouldn't freak out and then attempted to calibrate the proper amount of squeezing. Was my pinky properly placed? Were my palms too sweaty? But after a while, I let myself relax, and it felt like a moment that had to be.

"One spot down," Jane quietly said. "Four to go."

Which to me meant I'd already guaranteed at least the next four dates.

138 DAYS AFTER

THE CARROT AND THE STICK

Now it almost feels like that night happened to someone else, one of those memories where you see yourself from the outside, peering through a doorway at another life. I can't believe that was me.

The stairs creak. "Ray, dinner!"

"Not now," I yell. One of the problems with being in high school is that your parents tend to think of you as a plant that needs watering.

My mom remains standing on the stairs. I imagine her holding the railing tightly, trying not to blow up at me.

"Take a deep breath," I say, trying to annoy her, then kind of hating myself for it.

I hear her begin walking again, the footsteps becoming louder as she approaches my room. Picture the T. rex scene in *Jurassic Park*, where the water in the glass starts to ripple.

She knocks on the door.

"I'm not here," I say.

"I'm coming in," she says, more forcefully than usual.

"I'm naked!" I yell.

"No, you're not. You're sitting at your computer."

"Do you have cameras in here?"

"That's all you do lately," she snaps.

I see the doorknob turn just as I remember that I forgot to lock the door. My mom bursts through, a scowl on her face. "Ray, this is getting ridiculous."

She surveys the room. Water bottles strewn around, a graveyard of my last week's meals, my dresser and closet in the process of throwing up my entire wardrobe.

"You can't live like this," she says.

I take a deep breath, weighing my options.

Today in history—pretty much the only class I can almost pay attention in—Mr. Hillman taught us about a type of diplomacy called the carrot and the stick. It comes from the barbaric practice of placing a carrot in front of a mule to get it to walk. It's kept just out of reach so the mule is forever chasing this one measly carrot. As if that wasn't cruel enough, someone also starts to beat the mule. Since teachers are always telling us to apply what we learn in school to real life, I figured I'd try out this technique on my mom.

"You're right," I tell her, a smile pasted across my face. "I can't live like this. I love you, Mom."

The carrot.

She stops, caught off guard. "You do?"

"Of course I do."

Rich would call this progress.

"But if you don't get out of my room right now, I'm going to start throwing things."

The stick.

She glares at me, but instead of saying anything, she turns, marches out the door, and slams it.

Okay, I could have handled that better. It's just that everything in my brain is all twisted up.

It's like I can only move backward. But Jane's not really there either. Just the memory of a person I guess I didn't know as well as I thought.

206–205 DAYS BEFORE

THE FOLK WILLIAMSBURG FESTIVAL

Soon after Halloween, while we were eating lunch in the cafeteria, Jane invited us over to have dinner with her parents, though she somehow made it seem like a punishment. "Feel free to say no," she said, looking down at her plate, "but my parents want you guys to come over for dinner. They keep bugging me about it. I don't think I can take another reference about the Three Musketeers, Stooges, or Amigos."

By then, we were hanging out almost every day. The list of Burgerville sites remained in my backpack, but neither one of us seemed intent on finishing too quickly, as if finishing would make us define what we were outside the realm of Burgerville's history. We weren't ready to be labeled. Not yet.

We'd "study" together at the library, watch movies, or just spend hours talking. Those days were my favorite, when the three of us would lose ourselves in conversation about anything that popped into our heads.

"You actually believe the unibrow is a form of natural selection?" Jane asked me during one of our talks.

"Hear me out," I said. We'd just finished a unit on Darwinism in biology, where Mr. Parker had compared the process of natural selection to the comic book *Ant-man*. "Your forehead's kept warmer and it conveys power."

"Says who?"

"Simon told me."

"And who told Simon?"

"My mom," Simon said. "After I accidentally shaved off half of my eyebrow."

"I'll tweeze for you," Jane said.

"Thanks. I'm also thinking about waxing my chest."

"That sounds like a job for Ray," Jane said.

Jane and I also started to work together on school assignments for Mr. Parker; I'd suddenly discovered a newfound love for science—and explaining the terms to Jane.

"Why do you try so hard?" she asked me while we were studying together at the library.

"When the zombie apocalypse comes, I have to have something to offer."

Jane smirked. "You mean your brute strength isn't enough?"

I flexed and Jane felt my biceps, maintaining her grip a few seconds after I'd finished flexing. I swallowed hard. It wasn't quite second base, but at least the ball was in play.

"Keep studying," she said.

We even coordinated our Halloween costumes to go trick-or-treating with each of us dressing up as a different conspiracy theory: Simon wore an astronaut suit to commemorate the "fake" Apollo moon landing, I donned a reptile mask in honor of the reptilian elite that secretly control the world, and Jane dressed the same as she always did—all black—with the addition of a black cone on her head to personify the magic bullet in the assassination of JFK. To complete the outfit, she brought along a magic wand. Of course, nobody got it. Someone even thought she was a character from Harry Potter.

So when Jane invited us over for dinner, it felt important, another step in a friendship that had quickly become a defining moment in our lives. Simon could barely contain his excitement. "They want to meet us?" he asked, surprised. He began to list the things he could potentially bring—a dip, one of his grandfather's war medals that had been buried before the government could take it away, maybe even a gallon of milk, his own version of a bottle of wine.

"We're trying to be nice to each other," Jane said, making eye contact with me before quickly returning her gaze to the plate. "My parents and me."

I nodded. "Is it like a shirt and tie sort of event?"

"A shirt would be a good idea," she said.

"This isn't prom," Simon said. "Will there be time for pictures, though?"

"It's not a big deal," Jane said. "Actually, you know what? Let's forget the whole thing. Maybe another time."

"You can't do that," Simon said. "We've already cleared our schedules."

Jane thought for a while, weighing the pros and cons. "Okay, fine," she finally said. "How about tomorrow night?"

Simon and I quickly agreed.

Jane let out a deep breath and shrugged. "Here goes nothing."

The bell rang and Jane left to go to class. Simon and I walked to our last period trying to guess what her parents would be like.

"I bet her dad owns a chain of Italian restaurants and her mom was Miss America," Simon said.

"What about this," I said. "Her mom's family invented the glue stick and her dad spends his time doing a form of art using only his butt cheeks."

"Nice. Wait, how about this. Her mom's a doctor and her dad works on Wall Street."

"That's very probable, Simon."

"It sounded funnier in my head."

"I got it," I said. "Her mom's a witch doctor and her dad was in the movie *Wall Street*."

Simon adjusted his glasses. "I killed the joke."

We stopped in front of Simon's chemistry class.

"Are you nervous?" I asked.

"A little," he whispered.

I paused to let the moment sink in. We had never been worth having over for dinner before. Sure, we'd been invited to a couple of birthday parties, the play date with meal provided, the reluctant parent who bought me popcorn. But this was a night devoted to *us*. It felt like we graduated from middle school and found our way into Harvard.

"It's just a dinner," I said.

The rumors had died down about our little trio. There were still whispers, but for the most part, no one really bothered us. I felt triumphant; Jane had chosen us and the universe had bent to accommodate this new twist in reality. The only wrinkle in the plan was that we hadn't changed. Simon was still hopelessly naïve and a little too obsessed with tween vampire books. I was still me, a collection of stories without a story of my own.

"Are you bringing the milk or am I?" Simon asked.

"Is everything milk with you?" I snapped.

Simon looked wounded, lowering his gaze to the ground like a sad puppy.

"Sorry," I said.

Simon remained staring at his shoes.

"You bring the milk," I said.

He lifted his head. "Great, pick you up at seven."

The next night, Simon picked me up in the minivan and we made our way over to the New York Strip. It was dark by the time we left, and because there were hardly any streetlights in Burgerville, it felt like we were flying through space. I'd decided to bring a plate of cookies made by my mom to go along with Simon's milk, which was proving to be a major test of willpower. Luckily, trying not to eat any was helping me focus on something other than my nerves.

Once we got to the Strip, I noticed a lot of the houses already had Christmas lights up. Even Christmas came early for Burgerville's elite.

"What do you think of my tux?" Simon asked, referencing the T-shirt he wore replete with bow tie and ruffles graphic.

"Classy," I said.

I had decided on a loose-fitting collared shirt I found when raiding my mom's closet. Before my mom's trip to the Goodwill, most of my dad's clothes remained in a dark corner dubbed "his side," pants, shirts, and jackets collecting dust like a museum exhibit about the way things used to be. It'd been that way for almost two years. Meanwhile, my most recent growth spurt had opened up an entire new realm of fashion possibilities. While I was excited that I could finally wear his corduroy blazer, it also made me think about how much time had passed since I'd last seen him.

When we made our way onto Jane's street, Simon slowed down to look for her house number, which Jane had shared with us as if revealing classified information from a secret government dossier. She lived on the type of street where you could see the mailbox, but the houses were far out of sight, behind iron gates and stone walls.

"That's it!" Simon said.

We pulled in front of an iron gate that would have been more at home around a castle. I think both Simon and I thought the same thing. If Jane lived in a castle, who were we: knights in shining armor or enemy invaders?

Simon opened the window and reached out to press the button on the intercom.

"They're watching," I said, trying to lighten the mood.

"*Who's* watching?"

We heard a beeping noise as the gate magically swung open.

Simon's face went pale, as if he'd seen a ghost. He pressed the gas and inched forward.

The driveway was long and winding, with evergreen trees on either side. "Dude, she's rich," Simon said.

"No shit."

By the time the house came into full view, I was sweating profusely. I aired out my collar, not because it made any difference, but because I had seen it done in movies when characters were anxious. Simon did the same thing with his T-shirt. Emulating Jane, I said, "Here goes nothing."

We walked up the steps to the doorway. I expected to see a statue of a lion or some mythical beast, but the house itself was pretty understated. Maybe a little bigger than most, with a few extra flourishes like the intercom, but for the most part it wasn't all that different from a regular house.

The door swung open just as we reached it. Simon and I looked at each other, slightly freaked out by the Does' uncanny ability to anticipate our next move.

But the person who answered the door wasn't what we'd expected. "You made it," Mrs. Doe said excitedly. She wore a dress and a string of pearls around her neck. At least that's how I remember her that night. Something about her screamed *wholesome*, like she belonged in the 1950s: black-and-white, a manicured lawn, and a white picket fence, while her husband smoked a cigar.

"Come in," she said. The door opened wide, revealing a brightly lit foyer.

Like the astronauts of the fake moon landing, we timidly stepped through the doorway, afraid gravity might suddenly change. A chandelier hung high overhead and a portrait of an old lady stared at us from the stairwell. "My mother, Irene," Mrs. Doe said, following our gaze to the portrait. Dressed in black like her granddaughter, Irene had that same look of confusion Jane had when I first saw her in Mr. Parker's class, only sadder, like she'd never found what she was looking for.

"So who's Ray and who's Simon?" Mrs. Doe said, pointing at us. "No, wait, let me guess," she added cheerfully. She glanced down at the gallon of milk in Simon's hands, the label facing her as if it were a bottle of wine.

"It's whole milk," Simon said. "From a very expensive farm in New York."

"You must be Simon," Mrs. Doe said without missing a beat.

Simon nodded and handed her the milk, delicately placing it in her hands like a newborn baby.

"Which means you must be Ray." Mrs. Doe stared at me a second too long. She threaded her fingers through the handle on the milk, and with her free hand, took the plate of cookies from me.

"Scott, they're here," she yelled to the kitchen.

From across the room, we heard a quiet motor humming. Mr. Doe eventually revealed himself, riding on top of a motorized scooter. He was bald, but not in the weak nerd way, more like in the all-powerful Mr. Clean sort of way. He drove up next to us.

"Forgive me if I don't get up," he said, smiling.

"Ray," I said, putting out my hand.

He grabbed my hand and squeezed. Hard. I considered the possibility that every bone in my hand might now be broken and I would have to make it through dinner in severe pain, my fingers bent and twisted.

Simon approached Mr. Doe's chair and reluctantly extended his hand, having noticed the look of pain on my face during our introduction. At the last second, Simon balled his hand into a fist. Mr. Doe smiled and the two of them fist-bumped.

Just then Jane came to the stairs.

"There's still time to leave," she said when she reached the bottom step.

Mrs. Doe shook her head and rolled her eyes, the same way Jane would have.

"Who's hungry?" Mr. Doe asked. He turned his scooter and started toward the kitchen. We followed. I turned to look behind me and see how Jane was coping. All things considered, she seemed to be in a good mood, especially given how reluctant she was to have us over.

On our way to the kitchen, I tried to find pictures of Jane as a little kid, something with braces, or, even better, a picture of her riding in one of those pretend cars. But no such luck. Instead of putting their life on display the way most families do, it seemed to be locked away, the question of their past hidden in a few pieces of abstract art and phallic-inspired sculptures similar to my fourth-grade masterpiece (unless everything looks phallic to me, in which case I should probably bring this up to Rich). Scattered in between there was an odd assortment of clues, including a sign that said *The Does, Est. 1994,* and the portrait of Grandma Irene, of course.

We made small talk in the kitchen before taking our seats at a long wooden table in the dining room.

I was surprised to learn that Mrs. Doe was actually from Burgerville. "A hundred years ago," she said.

"She escaped," Jane added.

"It's not a prison," Mr. Doe said.

"It sure feels like one."

"It used to be a mental institution," I said, referencing the old McCallen Mansion where A. J. McCallen, Burgerville's founder, first opened his doors to those in need of help.

We were still on the first course, some sort of cold soup that had the consistency of glue.

"Used to be?" Jane asked.

"Maybe it still is and we just don't know it," Simon said.

"Back then, they really didn't know how to deal with mental illness," Mrs. Doe said.

Out of the corner of my eye, I saw Jane give her mom a look, the kind you give your parents when you're warning them not to bring out the photo albums or talk about your old imaginary friend.

"Well, I love it here," Mr. Doe said to fill the empty space. "I've never felt more free." He must have thought we didn't believe him, because he added, "Seriously, I do."

"When did you leave Burgerville?" I asked Mrs. Doe.

"A few years after the Folk Williamsburg Festival," she said. "I was just a baby."

I slurped the last of my soup, confused. There was no chapter of Burgerville's history I hadn't heard before. I pushed my bowl away and began mentally scanning through all of the detritus of the town's past—a long list of strange stories, crazy characters, and oddly colored animals. But I couldn't remember ever hearing about a folk music festival.

"You must know about the festival?" Mrs. Doe said in disbelief.

I shook my head.

"They don't teach that in school? It completely changed Burgerville."

Mr. Doe grabbed our bowls, preparing us for the next course.

"Jane's grandma organized the whole thing," Mrs. Doe said. "Back in the sixties she was one of the most respected folk singers in the country. How do you boys feel about folk?"

"I love it," Simon said. "The folkier, the better."

I agreed, not wanting to admit that I couldn't even name one folk song. "Folkadelic," I added.

"That's good to hear. You've got to have a big heart to like folk. What was that your friends in Brooklyn listened to?" she said to Jane.

"EDM," Jane said.

"Sounds like a medical condition," Mr. Doe said.

Jane gave him a stern look, which Mr. Doe took as a cue to continue. "Sorry, I can't come to work today. My EDM is acting up."

Jane covered her mouth to hide her laugh. "It stands for Electronic Dance Music," she said.

"Sure it does," Mr. Doe said, making his way back to the kitchen while mumbling in the voice of one of those medicine infomercials: "If you suffer from EDM . . ."

"Anyway," Mrs. Doe said, laughing, "my mother never quite made it to the level of a national headliner. She was known, but mostly by other musicians. One day, she decided she'd had enough of the New York scene and moved back to her hometown, Burgerville."

"The place where dreams go to die," Jane said.

"You know Simon and I grew up here, right?" I asked her.

"So you never had any dreams to begin with." She made a sarcastic face, as if to say *zing*.

In an attempt to flirt, I made the same face back at her, but judging from Jane's reaction, went past sarcastic and contorted my face into something you might see in a horror movie.

"But when she moved back," Mrs. Doe continued, "she realized the town was stuck in the fifties. No one was protesting the war. The kids were still wearing collared shirts and khakis. Women were stuck at home doing the cooking and cleaning. That's when my mother realized she needed to bring Burgerville into the new decade. She called some of her friends from the city and they put on a big concert right in the middle of Green Cow Acres. Burgerville was never the same. I can't believe they don't teach that in school."

I shrugged. "Roger Lutz doesn't even talk about it."

"That surprises me," Mrs. Doe said.

"You know Roger Lutz?" Jane asked her mom.

"Everyone knows Roger Lutz," Mrs. Doe said. She glanced back to the kitchen. "I better go help in there." She got up, placed her napkin on the table, and walked away.

The three of us sat in silence. I struggled to create a new image of Jane out of everything I had seen in the past hour. Her family was so completely . . . normal. Jane's annoyance at her mother's stories, her father's corny jokes. The only unanswered question was *why*. Why had the Does come back?

Jane picked up my napkin and placed it on my lap. She brushed my arm. My heart started racing.

"Where are your manners?" she said.

"Your parents seem really cool," Simon said to Jane.

Apparently that wasn't what Jane wanted to hear. She cringed. "Maybe they'll consider adopting you."

"I'm too old," he said, making it sound like a rebuttal.

"What about you, Ray?" Jane asked.

I began to fidget with my napkin. "What do you mean?"

"Your parents, you never talk about them."

"We have a mutual agreement," I said, taking a sip of water.

The scooter hummed, growing louder as Mr. Doe rolled in carrying two plates with a hamburger and fries on each.

"None of you are vegetarians, right?" he asked.

"It's against the law," I said, seriously. An old statute no one had ever bothered to change.

I looked down at my burger, my mouth watering. I took a bite and as I began chewing, noticed the entire table staring at me, their hands folded in front of their chins.

"We say grace, Ray," Mrs. Doe said.

"Right," I said through a mouth full of chewed burger. And out of the corner of my eye, I saw something that surprised me. Jane had her eyes closed and her hands folded.

We finished our dinner, had dessert—my mom's chocolate chip cookies and Simon's milk—and then said our good-byes to Jane's parents. Simon and I profusely thanked Mr. and Mrs. Doe for their hospitality.

"No thanks necessary," Mr. Doe said, his voice booming in the entryway.

Mrs. Doe, her voice barely a whisper compared to Mr. Doe's, said we were always welcome. Then Mr. Doe heaved himself off his scooter and onto an electrical escalator chair. He slowly ascended the stairwell, saluting Simon and me as he gained altitude.

"We'll be upstairs," Mrs. Doe said, "but you're welcome to stay until your curfew." She began to climb the stairs, careful to stay a few paces behind her husband.

The steely eyes of Grandma Irene watched us from the top of the stairwell. If she really was a hippie visionary, I wondered why she looked more like a mortician than a music festival pioneer.

We stayed for a couple of hours, watching TV in the family room. The occasional footsteps could be heard above, as well as Mrs. Doe's voice calling down the stairs, asking if we needed any refreshments.

Jane began flipping through the channels, the sound coming in bursts of chaotic noise.

Simon was the first to ask about Jane's father's disability.

"He's just lazy," Jane said.

It seemed almost like a nervous tic, the way she kept changing the channel, barely stopping to see what was on. She'd stop channel surfing only to talk.

"He's paralyzed," Jane added soon after, stating the obvious. An infomercial of someone selling a vacuum cleaner played in the background.

"Has he always been like that?" Simon asked.

"No," Jane said. She seemed to withdraw into herself, the remote clenched tightly in her hand as she kept her gaze focused on the TV.

A barrage of light pierced the darkness before Jane momentarily stopped on a scene from a romantic comedy.

"I don't talk to my dad," I said.

Our conversation mirrored the flashing mosaic of images on the TV. No connection, no continuity, just random snippets of conversation followed by losing ourselves in a tangle of thoughts.

"I caught my parents having sex once," Simon said in a sad tone.

Jane took her finger off the remote, landing on a cartoon of two animals speaking to each other, then resumed her channel surfing once again.

The light vibrated and transformed the dark room: a disco ball that could change color on demand, giving the room a surreal quality, dreamlike in its intensity. It felt like anything could happen.

I was sitting next to Jane on the couch. Simon lay on the loveseat, his feet propped over the edge. Eventually we heard a faint snore coming from him.

Jane and I drifted closer to each other. By the time I realized what had happened, our legs were touching.

Jane turned the TV off. The silence made all the other noises overpowering. The ticking of the grandfather clock. The pacing upstairs. Simon's snoring. A symphony of the everyday sounds of the night brought to the level of magic simply because we now paid attention to them. Our breathing added to the mix, a driving rhythm beneath the makeshift orchestra.

"Thanks for coming," Jane said.

I could feel her looking at me. I continued to stare straight ahead.

"Thanks for having me," I said, repeating the same dull line I'd learned to say since I was a kid.

"My grandmother didn't have such a happy ending," Jane said.

"Really?" I asked.

"Yeah, we used to listen to music together. She'd show me Pete Seeger, Hendrix, the Beatles. We'd play her old records. But after my grandpa died, she refused to come out of her room. Wouldn't eat. She didn't last much longer after that."

"I'm sorry," I said.

Jane shrugged.

The orchestra swelled. Like one of those cheesy commercials, the sounds seemed to be interconnected, the footsteps, the ticking, the snoring, our breathing, all forming a musical whole.

"What's your biggest secret?" Jane asked, whispering as if telling me a secret herself.

"I don't know."

"There must be something. Something you've done that you wish you could take back."

So much of my life was telling Burgerville's secrets, I hadn't thought to collect any of my own.

"Besides the time Simon and I made out?" I said, trying to lighten the mood.

"Darn," Jane said. "I was hoping to be your first."

The symphony momentarily disappeared. I turned to look at her, willing myself to lean forward. History always made everything seem so inevitable. But it really wasn't. Lips didn't come together on their own.

I swallowed hard, trying to convince myself to just go for it. But before I could work up the courage, Jane moved closer, so close I couldn't really see her.

"You really think all that stuff you say about history applies to life?" she said. "Like if you understand it better, it somehow changes things?"

I nodded. "I think so. We choose which parts to focus on. We exaggerate some, and leave other parts out. But the more stuff we include, the truer it becomes."

Jane seemed to think about this for a while.

"What got you so interested in history, anyway?" she asked.

"When I was little," I said, "my dad would take me to the Burgerville Library and we'd look at old pictures of people in the town archives and make up stories about their lives. It was kind of our thing. All of these long-dead shopkeepers, farmers, blacksmiths, you name it. We'd ignore all of the mayors and councilmen, and tell the history of Burgerville from their perspective. Ever since then, I've been hooked."

"Do you miss him?" Jane asked.

"I guess."

"Maybe someday you can write my history," Jane said quietly.

"You should write your own."

We sat in silence for what felt like hours. I turned to look at her. Her eyes were closed and her breathing had calmed to a gentle rise and fall. I put a cushion under her head and took one of the blankets strewn across the couch and draped it over her.

I went to shake Simon, but his eyes were already open, staring at the ceiling. I motioned toward the front door and we tiptoed out of the room.

We stopped in front of the stairs, the piercing eyes of Grandma Irene peering down at us.

I held her gaze, feeling the weight of her sadness.

Simon and I walked out into the cool night. The fresh air filled my lungs and I gulped it in.

"They loved us," Simon said as we made our way to the mini-van. "I couldn't have done it without you," he added, as if making a speech at an award show.

I patted him on the back. "You too."

A full moon hung high overhead, making it seem like there was a spotlight on us. Simon practically skipped to the van, jumping into the driver's seat, the engine rumbling to life as I lingered outside.

I turned to take one last look at the Does' house and found myself thinking that maybe a lot more than green cows lay beyond the horizon.

155 DAYS AFTER

NOTABLE EVENTS FROM THIS WEEK IN SCHOOL

1) Mr. Hillman gave a lecture on the merits of isolationism. It started off strong, then became a diatribe against his ex-wife for being distant in their marriage even though he was the "perfect husband."

2) Mr. Parker stopped me in the hallway to ask me how I was doing with "everything." When I told him I was doing "fine"—I find it best to be as vague as possible—he gave me a long list of comic books to read that helped him through difficult times in his life, most notably the death of his parents, and by *his parents*, I mean Batman's parents.

3) Harold Ronkowski, who I haven't talked to since middle school, cornered me at the urinal and wanted to talk about how I was doing. "I know we're not friends," he said, "but I'm around if you want to talk." Unfortunately, Harold didn't abide by the look-straight-ahead rule when peeing, so it was extremely awkward. "I'm fine," I told him. "It's not your fault," he said. I flushed and walked away.

4) I got a text message in the middle of chemistry, and for the whole class I couldn't shake the feeling that it was from Jane. I

know, it's crazy, but I fully expected to look at the phone and see Jane's name, some text about going to see another crazy Burgerville landmark or a line from one of her favorite folk songs. Instead it was my mom: *Have a great day!* At first I just said, *No,* but then I felt kind of guilty, so I added a winky-face emoji.

5) Simon's shoes ran out of batteries. "They haven't heard the last of me," he said when the lights finally went out during lunch. "I'm definitely considering writing a strongly worded letter." But then he looked down at his plate, a collection of every dairy product imaginable, and said, "I probably won't. But I'm sending very negative energy their way."

6) My dad called me. He'll do that from time to time. He didn't leave a voicemail or anything. I guess after over two years of not speaking, we're not really at voicemail-familiar. More like dental-postcard-reminder. After he moved to Florida and I saw how upset my mom was, I guess I didn't have much to say to him. Well, I have things to say to him now, but they're not the kind of things you'd write on a postcard.

7) I made this list based on Rich's recommendation to "catalogue meaningful events in your life."

193–192 DAYS BEFORE

SIMON'S LAW

Simon and I only realized how much our lives had changed when Jane went to Pennsylvania to celebrate Thanksgiving with her relatives. It was like being given fire, then having it taken away after only a couple of months. Jane seemed upset by her forced departure, as if she was spending the holiday on a small island in the middle of nowhere—surrounded by cannibals.

"I can't believe I'm saying this," she said during biology, "but I wish I was staying in Burgerville."

"Weird relatives? Extra limbs? War criminals?"

"Not exactly. It just brings back bad memories."

I thought of my own family trips, the nonsensical fights about directions or where to eat, my dad occasionally threatening to walk home no matter the distance. All the signs of a healthy, functional family.

"Whenever I get upset about something, I just think of the most random image possible. It kind of makes you lose track of whatever's getting you down." It was a strategy I'd been developing ever since my dad left.

Jane narrowed her eyes.

"Seriously, it works. So if you're getting annoyed with your family, just think about"—I paused, trying to come up with a good one—"a polar bear riding a scooter . . . Oh, and the bear's completely hairless."

Jane smiled. "Nice touch."

"Okay, now you try."

Jane thought for a little while. "I think I got it. Mr. Parker dressed as Batman casually eating a burrito."

I laughed. "That's a little too realistic. We'll work on it."

At the front of class, Mr. Parker continued to ramble on about the intersection of comic books and biology: "Who can tell me why Storm from the *X-Men* might have been born with mutated genes?"

Everyone in class looked down at their notebooks. "Okay, I want you to pair, care, and share," he said, basically a ten-minute talking break with a twist—everyone had to say one nice thing about their partner before trying to figure out what the hell Mr. Parker was talking about.

I thought about all of the things I could say to Jane. *You've made everything in Burgerville better. You're the kind of beautiful that makes the word* beautiful *seem stupid. You remind me of spring and fall and chocolate chip cookies.* But I was too nervous to actually say any of them. I finally settled on something more low stake. "I like your shirt," I said. It was another one of her obscure folk tees, this one advertising some sort of Folktacular that had occurred in Brooklyn.

"Three days of hardcore acoustic folk," Jane said.

"Your turn," I said.

She looked like she was going through her own list of compliments, but I guess she wasn't ready to share her list either.

"You still have all your hair," she said.

On Thanksgiving Day, Simon and I went with my mom to a homeless shelter to serve Thanksgiving dinner, a tradition started after my dad left. I guess my mom was trying to make sure I became a good person. And that I didn't turn into a selfish, egotistical asshole like my dad. At least that's what I heard her say on the phone once.

The shelter was located in the city of Murphy. Unfortunately for Murphy, it had the highest poverty rate in the county, the highest crime rate, and *Burgerville County Magazine* had rated it "The worst place to drive through" nine out of the past ten years.

Every year, when we crossed the border into Murphy, Simon and I would look for the sign that let us know we arrived. Years ago, some vandal had gone the extra mile and given the city a slogan that fully warned any visitors of the truth about their upcoming destination.

"There it is," Simon said excitedly.

"They still haven't changed it," I said.

The sign featured the name Murphy written in big white letters on a blue background, with the city emblem underneath, a coat of arms made up of two cows being balanced on the scales of justice. Scrawled across the bottom in black bold letters, someone had written: *Whatever can go wrong, will go wrong.*

Although they were spray-painted, it felt like the words had been written into the very character of the city.

"Murphy's Law," I said.

"Whatever can go wrong, will go wrong," Simon said gravely.

We arrived at the homeless shelter a little bit past three o'clock and immediately started working. Simon and I put on our hairnets and finished up preparing the food, stirring massive cauldron-sized pots of stuffing, basting turkeys with kitchen utensils that could have doubled as squirt guns (and momentarily did), and putting slices of pumpkin pie on small plates.

My mom stood across the kitchen talking to a man I had never seen before. They were both wearing aprons, putting the final touches on a gigantic mound of mashed potatoes.

"That guy looks like Superman," Simon said.

"In an apron," I said.

"No, that's his cape. It's just turned around."

My mom caught me looking at her and motioned for me to come over.

I approached hesitantly.

"This is my friend Tim," she said.

He took off his plastic glove and we shook hands.

I looked at my mom suspiciously. The idea of her having a friend was strange. For the past two years, she seemed to exist only as an extension of my life: picking me up from school, making dinner, bothering me to do my homework. I could only imagine her as a mom.

"I've heard a lot about you," Tim said.

"Why?"

Tim struggled for words, glancing at my mom.

"I brag about you all the time," she quickly said.

"For what?" I asked.

I hold no illusions about myself. I don't play any sports, I don't have straight A's, I'm not in any clubs, and probably my most notable accomplishment is winning my eighth-grade spelling bee. I guess what I'm trying to say is there's not much to brag about.

My mom's face went flush and I realized I'd embarrassed her. I didn't know if it was because she didn't have an answer to my question or if she was just uncomfortable with her new role as "not just a mom." I felt like I'd discovered her secret identity.

"Get back to work, Ray," my mom said, stirring the potatoes.

As I made my way across the room, Simon looked at me funny. "What was that all about?"

"I don't know."

"Is that her boyfriend?"

"What? No, of course not. It's her friend."

"Women and men can't be friends."

"Jane's our friend."

"But we both want her to be our girlfriend."

"You do?" I said, more angrily than I intended.

"Relax. I'm just making a point. But if you died fulfilling your dream of cage diving with great white sharks, I'd certainly try."

For some reason, that calmed me.

"What's Jane up to, anyway?" Simon asked.

I took out my phone and smiled when I saw that Jane had sent me a few texts. In one, there was a link to an article about a chupacabra sighting in Connecticut; according to the author, the mythological creature had migrated from Central America as a result of global warming. In another text, clearly inspired by my random image technique, Jane had written: *Bigfoot protesting a parking ticket.*

"I hope I can find a girlfriend," Simon said as he watched me texting Jane back. I took a picture of Simon in his hairnet and sent it to Jane with the caption: *Simon wearing a hairnet. You're welcome.* It wasn't until after I sent the text that the full weight of Simon's words hit me. While we hadn't made anything official, hadn't even kissed, it was definitely a good sign. Maybe my wish was coming true.

We took turns spooning out clumps of food to the people lined up. Murphy's Law could be seen in all of their faces; each person had their own story to tell. For the first time since I'd been going, I actually felt like I was making a little difference. I guess my mom's social engineering was working.

Everything was going great until I noticed my mom and Tim across the room. Talking, laughing, taking a break together—they were having fun! The final straw came when Tim playfully tapped my mom on the arm and leaned in to whisper something in her ear. Needless to say, I was appalled.

"I think you're right," I said to Simon once the line had died down.

"About what?"

"My mom. I think she likes that guy."

"That's good," Simon said.

"Why would that be good?"

"Maybe she'll be happy. What's the worst thing that could happen?"

I had visions of Tim moving in, me being forced to call him Dad, then being sent off to boarding school, because hey, isn't that what all evil stepparents do?

"You don't really think your mom is gonna date Superman, do you?" Simon asked after we'd finished cleaning up, a hint of jealousy in his tone.

"No," I said. "Well, maybe. Whatever *can* go wrong, *will* go wrong."

"What if it's the opposite?" he asked. "And whatever can go right, *will* go right?"

"Simon's Law?"

"I'm totally posting that on the internet."

"I hope it catches on."

On our way back, no mention was made of Tim. It felt like we were all in the car and somewhere else at the same time, a thought made eerie by our reflections in the windows. The bright lights of Murphy made our reflections look like they were alternate versions of ourselves. They drove beside us, judging us from a distance, maybe from another dimension.

"It's time," my mom said, referring to our tradition of saying one thing we were thankful for on the way home.

"I'll start," Simon said. Disembodied Simon sat quietly in the window, waiting for real Simon to speak.

"I'm thankful to be part of this family," Simon said.

Kiss-ass. Simon always knew how to suck up to my mom.

"That's very sweet, Simon."

"Even though it's technically false," I said.

My mom shook her head. "What about you?"

"I'm thankful Simon's *not* part of the family," I said.

"Ouch."

"Be serious," my mom said.

"Fine. I'm thankful that this year is different." Almost as if on cue, my phone buzzed. It was another message from Jane: *Earl Beddington dressed like a cowboy riding on a green cow.* Jane must have been having a tough time in Pennsylvania. I quickly texted back: *Nice. But maybe a different outfit for Beddington? A mankini?*

A silence hung in the car. We approached the sign that said we were entering Burgerville. Someone had long ago crossed out *Williamsburg* and written *Burgerville* in bubble letters, sandwiched between an oversized sesame-seed bun.

"I'm going to eat so much, I might explode," Simon said. As was tradition, Simon would go eat with his family while my mom and I would find a diner somewhere and get anything *but* turkey. It just didn't feel right to have a whole Thanksgiving feast with only the two of us.

"What are you thankful for?" I asked my mom.

"I'm thankful for you and Simon."

"And?"

"And that this year is different."

Catching a glimpse of her reflection, I saw a smile begin to form, the type of mischievous grin that tells you you're only getting part of the truth.

172 DAYS AFTER

ROLE PLAYING

"If your parents were here right now, what would you say to them?"

Lately, Rich has been doing this thing where I have to play all the different people and emotions in my life. So I end up having to pretend I'm my mom or dad or Anger or even the cafeteria lady (she was a real jerk to me one day). And let me tell you, I make one hell of a nice lunch lady.

"Do we really have to do this?" I ask, having flashbacks to my fifteen minutes wearing a metaphorical hairnet.

"We can talk about something else if you like. How about we start with kindergarten?"

"You're good," I say. "Okay, here I go. How's Florida, Dad?"

Switching chairs.

"Awesome. It's always hot. I go to Disney World all the time."

Back to my chair.

"That's pretty weird, Dad."

Switch.

"Well, I have a new family. And cancer."

I love making shit up.

"Stick to the facts," Rich says.

Back to my chair.

"Why did you leave?" I ask, monotone.

Switch.

"Because your mother was driving me nuts."

"Now what would your mom say?" Rich says, rudely interrupting my conversation with my dad.

Switching to a different chair in the corner of the room.

"You're an asshole," my mom says, played by me.

"Who, me?" I say, running to my chair.

"Or *me*?" I say as I collapse into my dad's chair.

It feels like a workout sometimes.

I jump back into my mom's chair.

"You," she says, pointing at my dad.

"Ask her why she's so angry at your dad," Rich says.

"Because he left," I say, breaking character.

"No, ask *her*," Rich says.

"Because I'm all alone," I hear myself say.

I start to feel really guilty, so I jump up and go back to my chair.

"I'm sorry, Mom," I say. "But you can't dwell on the past."

"Tell *yourself* that," Rich says.

"That's just something you say to make people feel better. Like time heals all wounds or a stitch in time saves nine, whatever that means."

"It's worth a try."

"I feel like I'm being inducted into a cult."

"Repeat after me," Rich says. "I can't dwell on the past."

I roll my eyes, squirming in my chair, and repeat the words.

"Good, now drink this Kool-Aid," Rich says, completely deadpan.

He does have his moments.

189 DAYS BEFORE

SUPERMAN UNLEASHED

Simon's intuition proved to be right on about Tim, the homeless shelter Superman. He came over to help my mom move some furniture a few days after Thanksgiving. No, that isn't a euphemism for sex.

When I saw his car approach the driveway, my defenses immediately went up. Feeling mysteriously like a supervillain, I asked my mom what he was doing at our house.

She pointed to a couch in our family room. "Can you move that by yourself?"

I heard his car door close.

I walked over to the couch, bent over, and attempted to lift it. It came only a few inches off the ground before crashing down.

"You've won this time," I said.

The doorbell rang.

"Be nice," my mom said, before opening the door. Tim stood on the porch wearing glasses, jeans, work boots, and a red-and-blue nylon jacket with a white T-shirt underneath.

I didn't know what Simon was thinking calling him Superman. He may have had the colors down, but he looked more like a nerd trying to play construction worker. We shook hands, neither one of us revealing our secret identity: Tim's alter ego as Supernerd and mine as the supervillain Raynman. Yes, I know it sounds like the movie, but too bad.

"I think this room just needs a change," my mom said to Tim.

"What were you thinking?" Tim asked.

In my head, I added *little lady*, as in "What were you thinking, little lady?" Something about the way he spoke sounded wooden, like he was repeating lines he saw in a Western.

My mom laid out the plan for the move and Supernerd and I rolled up our sleeves. I went to one end of the couch and he went to the other. We both bent over, trying to grab hold of the bottom, but neither one of us could get a good grip. Super strength my ass.

"Give me a second," Tim said. He took off his glasses and jacket. Then his entire persona changed. His voice became deeper and his muscles seemed to bulge through his shirt.

My mom looked on in awe as Tim now easily lifted up his end of the couch. Breathing heavily, on the verge of defeat, I had no choice but to call in my mom for help. I held my head in shame, the first supervillain in the history of comic books to need his mother to fight his battles for him. Then it was the three of us, all of our effort going into moving the couch, the forces of light and dark banding together for the noble goal of interior design.

Tim placed the couch down, nodding solemnly as the legs touched the ground.

"Piece of cake," he said.

For the rest of the afternoon, I kept trying to find something wrong with Tim, the kryptonite that would make his superpowers disappear.

My mom ordered pizza and the three of us went into the kitchen to eat. Tim unknowingly sat in my dad's chair, which I almost said something about, but my mom gave me a preemptive look, one of those *grounded for life* type glares. I mustered as much telepathic hatred as I could, but it only appeared to make him stronger, a broad smile on his face as he told stories about his exploits saving the world in the Peace Corps. I could see right through his do-gooder résumé, but apparently my mom didn't have the same powers of X-Ray vision. She kept laughing real loud and leaning forward when he spoke. I knew she had fallen under his spell and I was the only one who could rescue her.

"Kids?" I asked him after he'd finished another long and boring story about his time helping people get clean water or democracy or cable TV.

He shook his head. "Just a dog. A golden retriever named Robin."

He had a sidekick!

"Ever married?" I asked, taking the last slice of pizza and staring Tim down.

My mom choked a little. "Ray!" she said.

"No, that's okay, [little lady]," Tim said. "The truth is, Ray, I've never found the right person."

"Have you ever been arrested?"

"Once."

Ha! The chink in the armor!

"It was at a Save the Dolphins rally. I got a little carried away," he said, laughing.

I thought of him cradling a dolphin in his arms as he walked onto shore, a crowd of onlookers holding their breath in anticipation as he gave Flipper CPR.

And then, as he was leaving, he asked me if I liked baseball.

"No," I said.

He seemed caught off guard. I hadn't given a shit about baseball for a couple of years. That was something my dad and I had done together. When he left, my interest in baseball went out the proverbial broken window.

Undeterred by my terse response, Tim pulled a signed baseball out of his jacket and threw it to me. "I thought you might like to have this," he said, as if reading a line of dialogue someone had forgotten to change.

"You love baseball, Ray," my mom said, part statement, part command.

I held the ball in my hand, reading the name I didn't recognize.

"I do?" I said. I tossed it in the air and caught it. Tim smiled and I thought about throwing it right at his stupid face.

Tim then launched into a story about how he got the ball, someone's record-breaking home run or something like that, and assured me it would be worth a lot of money someday.

"Thanks," I said, before chucking the ball onto the couch and going to the kitchen.

After he left, my mom seemed to be lost in thought. I wondered if she was mad at me, if I should have tried a little harder to like Tim. We stood over the sink doing dishes. I watched the little beads of soap collect and then disappear, thinking about how much had changed since my dad left. The past few months I felt like my mom and I were finally becoming a family again. We had left behind the people we were, thrown them in a scrapbook alongside the old day-to-day routines, the inside jokes and holiday rituals, the uncomfortable silences that followed a fight. When so much changes, you have no choice but to change yourself. The only question was whether or not we were okay with that. I certainly had misgivings. And now with this intruder, Tim, something just didn't feel right.

"How do you feel about the new setup in the family room?" my mom asked, waking me up from my dish meditation.

"I don't know. It's kind of boring."

"But there's something refreshing about its simplicity," she said.

"Yeah, but if I had to spend more than a couple of hours in there, I think I'd poke my eyes out."

She turned the faucet off.

"What are you talking about?"

"What are *you* talking about?"

"Is everything okay, Ray?"

I had gotten a little bit more worked up than I thought.

"It's just that I like the old family room," I said.

"Change is good, Ray. Otherwise, life is boring."

"*Tim's* boring," I blurted out.

"Give him a chance, Ray," she said. "People can surprise you."

I marched upstairs to my room, thinking about our upcoming comic book: *Superman vs. Raynman: The Element of Surprise,* a ten-issue opus about the chaos that ensues when Superman exacts his most twisted revenge yet: dating the villain's mother.

188–182 DAYS BEFORE

THE LOST WOODS

With Jane in the picture, though, I didn't have much time to worry about Tim or think about my dad. I was too focused on the now. Life had changed so much. Simon and I were officially no longer a couple of outcasts—with Jane, we were *the* group of outcasts, a deformed set of conjoined triplets that couldn't be separated.

"What's going on?" Simon said one afternoon.

"What do you mean?"

"It's like the spell has been broken."

"What spell?" Jane asked.

"I just assumed there was a spell," Simon said.

"So then I'm your fairy godmother?"

"Sort of," Simon said. "Only if I'm Cinderella."

"Then I guess I'm the prince?" I asked.

"You're the talking mouse," Simon corrected.

Jane tapped me on the head with her pencil, pretending to cast a spell. "Who says you can't be both?"

Later, Jane drew me a picture of the three of us together, Simon in a Cinderella dress, me as a mouse-prince hybrid, and her floating above as a somewhat demonic fairy godmother.

Even guys like Tommy Beddington seemed to look at me differently. For the first time since the pudding incident, he spoke to me. We were passing each other in the hallway, and as usual, I was staring at the ground in an attempt to avoid awkward hallway eye contact. All of a sudden, I heard Beddington's voice. "Hey, Ray," he said.

I thought I imagined it. After years of really only talking to Simon, it felt like one of those scenes from the movies where the ghost suddenly realizes someone can see them.

"Hey, Tommy," I said uncertainly. *Don't make a joke about the green cows. Don't make a joke about the green cows.*

He walked away, and I was left feeling like I'd suddenly earned entrance into another world.

That same week, Jane called me and asked if I wanted to go on a hike in the Lost Woods.

"It's time to cross another spot off the list," she said. She sounded serious, like it was some sort of religious obligation.

"I'm always ready to journey into Burgerville's history," I said. "Let me just see what Simon's up to."

"Maybe it should just be me and you today."

I almost dropped the phone. My brain couldn't process the sudden turn of events. I took a deep breath, trying my best to sound casual. "Oh, okay, yeah, sounds good, why not?" When Jane didn't say anything—I mean, was she supposed to? Or maybe I didn't give the proper response time?—I kept going: "Cool, I'm down, whatever"—Was I being enthusiastic enough?—"I'd *love* to go hiking with you."

I called Simon on the way over to ask for advice.

"She wants to go *hiking* with you?"

I heard a keyboard in the background.

"What are you doing?"

"I'm searching the internet to see if hiking is really code for 'let's go make out in the woods.'"

"And?"

"It just means hiking. Unless she said 'take a hike.' In which case you really misinterpreted her phone call."

"I think I'm in over my head."

Simon agreed.

"No, you're supposed to be giving me a pep talk. Tell me how great I am. To just be myself and have fun and all that stuff."

"Look, you've already gone way further than anyone would've ever predicted."

"Thanks?"

"I'll be honest, part of me thought that Jane might have befriended you because your mom was paying her off. I'm not proud of it, but I think now's the time to put all of our cards on the table. You're a nice guy and all, but the history stuff isn't for everyone, not to mention your acne has really flared up in the past few weeks and—"

"This isn't helping, Simon."

"What I'm saying is, this kind of thing doesn't happen every day for guys like us. Something weird has been going on these past few weeks. Maybe . . ."

"Simon's Law?"

"Dammit, Ray. Don't jinx it." Then, like he was reading off a cue card: "Just remember: You're great. Have fun and be yourself. Did I miss anything?"

"Thanks, Simon. I needed that."

"And if you do something really horrible like accidentally insult her mother or clog her toilet—I mean, I'm sure you'll do great— but if you do totally mess it up, try to subtly hint that I might like her too."

"Good talk," I said.

As I drove down Jane's driveway, the front door opened. Mr. and Mrs. Doe waited in the entrance.

I parked the car and thought about Simon's Law. Maybe it was just a question of perspective. The more you focused on the good things, the more you noticed them. And vice versa. I took a deep breath and got out of the car.

"There he is," Mr. Doe said as I made my way to the porch.

"The history buff," Mrs. Doe said.

As I walked inside, Grandma Irene greeted me from her perch at the top of the stairs, somehow looking even sadder than last time.

There were papers strewn about the family room. A large map of the world hung on the wall, red tacks poked through capitals with lines of string connecting them.

"Sorry about the mess," Mr. Doe said. "We're moving to Europe."

I had a mini panic attack as I tried to figure out what he meant. The Does were moving?

Mrs. Doe must have been able to read the expression on my face, because she quickly added, "Our company. Our company's going international."

"Thank god . . ." I accidentally said. I stretched out the end, trying to recover. ". . . That your company's doing so well. Praise the Lord."

"I didn't know you were so religious, Ray," Mr. Doe said.

"Might as well hedge your bets," I said.

Mr. Doe looked at me funny.

I coughed to take the attention off my awkwardness. "So what's your company do?"

"The short explanation, sweetie," Mrs. Doe said.

"So no PowerPoint?" He smiled. "Kidding. I'm kidding. I've always loved to travel, and they don't make it easy for . . ." His voice trailed off. I tried not to look at his legs. "Well, they don't make it easy for anyone. So a few years ago, I got together with some computer friends of mine and we created a website to help change that. All you have to do is answer a few questions about your trip and then our algorithms do the work. Put in info about allergies, kids, transportation needs, whatever, and then we create a personalized itinerary based on information from other users. And it's always being updated. Kind of like Waze, but for vacationing."

"But we were first," Mrs. Doe said.

"And our app just won an award from the Travel Channel," Mr. Doe said.

"Wow," I said.

Jane appeared beneath her grandmother's portrait, her heavy black boots thudding on the steps as she made her way down the stairs. She had on a flannel shirt and cargo pants. Outdoorsy Jane.

"Not the app," Jane said. "Anything but the app."

"It's going to change travel as we know it," Mr. Doe said confidently.

"I'm sure it will, but we only have so much daylight." Jane reached the bottom of the stairs. "And we've got a hike planned."

"Be careful out there," Mrs. Doe said. "It's really easy to get lost in the Lost Woods."

"Who would've thought," Jane said.

Outside, the sky was a pale gray. It looked like all the color had been scraped out of it.

Jane motioned to a path at the edge of her backyard where the lawn stopped. "Shall we?"

We walked along the path, journeying into the heart of the Lost Woods. The trees had already lost most of their leaves. The few remaining barely held on, and every so often, a breeze would send one of the final holdouts swirling in the air.

The path splintered in two directions. "Which way?"

"We don't have much of a choice," Jane said. "See?" She motioned to the path that forked left. There was a small wooden bridge a few yards ahead. The middle of the bridge was gone, two wooden ends with nothing in between. I walked closer. Jane joined me and together we stood at the edge.

Something flew across the water, the branches shaking, leaves scattering around us.

"The Flying Possum of Williamsburg," Jane said matter-of-factly.

"The what?" I thought back to the sweatshirt Jane was wearing the night we played Never Have I Ever.

"You don't know the story of the Flying Possum of Williamsburg?"

I shook my head.

"Damn."

"What are you talking about?"

"Ellie and I made it up. Back in Brooklyn. We'd seen so many ridiculous conspiracy theories spread around the internet, we decided to create one ourselves. We came up with this vicious flying possum engineered in a government lab in Brooklyn to help with the rodent infestation. And then we went to work. Started talking about it in public. Posted a few things on the internet. Ellie even had shirts and sweatshirts made. But so far, no luck."

"Taking after Earl Beddington, I see."

"Sort of. Except I don't actually believe there's a flying possum."

I stared at her.

"Okay, maybe just a tiny bit."

She turned to me and smiled, the same smile I saw on her first day of school, like she knew what I was thinking. And in that moment, I was thinking that I loved her—how everything she said was magnified, how I wanted to know her whole history, from the big events to the smallest details.

We slipped through a thicket of bushes to the other trail and walked in silence for a few minutes.

"Thanks for humoring my dad," Jane said. "Once he gets talking about the app, there's no stopping him. After his accident, he kind of got the travel bug."

"What happened?" I asked hesitantly.

Jane took a while to respond. We kept walking. The sound of leaves crunching underfoot. Puddles of light breaking up the shadows.

"It was a car accident," Jane finally answered. "I was only five years old. We were visiting my grandparents in Pennsylvania. There was this ice cream shop I loved and my dad promised he'd pick us up some after dinner. There was a bad storm, and I remember him saying we'd have to wait till tomorrow. Five-year-old Jane didn't like that, so he went anyway."

She lowered her gaze to the ground.

"You were just a kid," I said.

"Believe me, I've heard that a million times."

Jane began to walk faster. I matched her pace, trying to navigate the rocky terrain. My study of history was so objective, I'd sometimes forget how the past could haunt you. Of course, now I know.

We turned down yet another path. I got the distinct feeling that the woods were guiding us, turning us this way and that.

"These paths were used to send messages during the Revolutionary War," I said.

"Alert, alert," Jane said. "Historical anecdote coming."

"I didn't know you found my stories so exciting," I said. "But if you insist. During the Revolutionary War, one of the British soldiers, Colonel John Hutchinson, stumbled onto these paths. He couldn't wait to tell his superiors. He thought he was gonna be the reason the British won the war. But unfortunately for him, he ended up getting lost."

"And so let me guess . . . his spirit haunts the woods?"

"Not exactly. By the time they found him, the war was over, but the poor guy had already lost his mind, muttering about King George and the colonists, how everyone was going to be tarred and feathered, maybe hanged. His rescuers were so annoyed with him, they just left him there. Ever since then, the woods kind of got a bad reputation, partly because people thought the woods had special powers, but mostly because the trees are so thick, they block out most of the stars, the preferred navigation system for most of the nineteenth century."

"People don't like simple explanations," Jane said. "It kind of takes the magic out of life. No aliens, no ghosts, no magical woods, no green cows . . ."

"No flying possums," I said.

"I didn't say that," Jane said.

We reached a small clearing where six stones were arranged in a circle. It must have been an old campground. We sat down next to each other. Branches hung overhead, reaching into the gray, colorless landscape above.

Jane picked a leaf up off the ground and began tearing it into pieces. "So why don't you and your dad talk anymore?"

I sighed. The *why* was getting more and more confusing as time passed.

"The day he left, I came home and saw a bunch of suitcases by the door. He must have been rehearsing his good-bye speech for a while, because the second I walked in, he started spouting out all these cliché lines. Telling me that we'd still be a family. He loved me. I could visit him whenever I want. But the whole time he was talking, all I could really focus on was my mom. She was standing in the kitchen, just glaring at him. Every so often she'd let out this sound, kind of like a snort, but a bunch in a row, like she couldn't breathe. So instead of shaking his hand or hugging him before he left, I told him I didn't ever want to see him again."

I gazed up at the sky, listening to the sound of crickets grow louder, and then looked over at Jane, her eyes practically glowing in the dusk as she moved closer to me.

"It's stupid," I said. "I know a lot of people have it way worse."

"It's not a competition," she said.

"I know."

"Hey," Jane said. "The Abominable Snowman taking a selfie for his Facebook profile pic."

"Thanks," I said. "I already feel better."

Jane was tapping her foot, looking all around.

"Is everything okay?"

"There's something I have to show you," she said. She rolled up her sleeve and carefully peeled back her bracelets. I could see a thick scar.

"I don't want you to be freaked out," she said.

I held her wrist in my hand, staring down at the raised skin. I ran my finger over it. At first Jane's body jolted, like the wound was still open. But then I felt her relax. The skin was rough, craggy, torn up; holding her small wrist, I realized she wasn't invincible like I'd first thought.

"Promise me you'll never do that again," I said.

When Jane didn't say anything, I pulled her closer. "Jane?"

She shook her head. "I can't change what happened and I don't want to talk about it, but I really like you, and I don't want you to think of me any differently."

She really likes me. I tried to stay in the moment. "One thing doesn't define you. It's just part of the truth."

"I just want you to understand why I need to move slow." She slid her bracelets back over her scar.

I nodded. For someone who'd lived his whole life moving backward, slow felt like a hundred miles an hour. But still, there were a lot of things I didn't understand. That I still don't understand.

We held hands and sat there until dark, the gray sky turning a fiery shade of orange before the sun went down.

191 DAYS AFTER

BRAIN CLEANING

At my last session, Rich gave me another one of his "little steps" to take, an activity he calls "Brain Cleaning," a nice euphemism for brainwashing. I take a situation, record my response to it, and then think of a better, healthier response. Rinse and repeat.

Situation #1: I'm sitting at lunch with Simon when he starts talking about seeing his favorite vampire author speak. After an extremely long plot synopsis of one of her books—*Air Force Blood*, a dystopian novel about the president being a vampire—Simon steers the conversation into college talk, as if my mom's gotten to him, and the two of them are teaming up to get me to start filling out applications. After all, what college wouldn't want a spelling bee champ with at least three hours of community service under their belt?

My Response: I want to ask him how he can talk so much about the future, about a world without Jane, but instead I say, "Can we change the subject?"

And he says, "Sure, I just thought—"

But I interrupt and say, "I don't want to hear about college."

And he asks, "Are you gonna drink your milk?"

And for some reason that bothers me, so I kind of slide the carton across the table and it spills.

And as the milk begins cascading onto the floor and Simon laps up whatever bit he can, I say, "I don't understand how you can talk about college."

And Simon says, "Jane would have wanted us to go to college."

And I say, "You don't have a clue what Jane wanted. Neither of us did." Then I storm off, into the historical dead zone of Mr. Hillman's class, to listen to him ramble on about how he somehow contributed to the fall of the Berlin Wall.

Brain Cleaning: I should have said, "I appreciate you trying to help, Simon, but I'm just not ready. It's like making plans for the future means I'm letting go of Jane and erasing our history together. And I'd love to give you my milk. You are, after all, still growing."

Situation #2: My dad leaves a voicemail on my phone. "Just calling to check in," he says. "Your mom's worried about you."

My Response: I consider throwing my phone against the wall. Instead, I run down the stairs and calmly tell my mom—okay, my voice may have been slightly raised—

to stop trying to fix me. And to leave my dad out of it. And maybe something about hating her. To which she responds, "He's your father."

And I say, "Then maybe he shouldn't have moved to Florida."

And she says, "He wanted a fresh start."

And then I say, even though I know I shouldn't have, "He left *you* too."

She glares at me, but only says, "I know you're just saying that because you miss her."

And I scream and run up the stairs.

Brain Cleaning: I should have written my dad a letter about how I appreciate his concern but I'm just not quite ready to talk yet. Maybe include a fun anecdote about playing catch and how the Yankees are doing and how Mom's dating Tim (okay, maybe leave that part out). And then I should have calmly walked down the stairs and had a frank discussion with my mom about teenage depression, how I'm trying to get better, and I appreciate all of her concern. And hey, maybe Tim and I can grab pizza sometime.

Situation #3: Rich gives me an assignment called "Brain Cleaning."

My Response: It feels like homework. And I'm not even doing homework for school, so I tell him, "This feels like I'm doing your job for you."

And he asks, "What if Brain Cleaning actually works?"

And I say, "Then you're going to have a lot of free time on your hands."

Brain Cleaning: I should have said, "Thank you, Rich, in your infinite wisdom for giving me this fun, yet educational activity. I'm sure this list will help me contend with life's big philosophical conundrums and I'll have you to thank for it."

181–168 DAYS BEFORE

THE OTHER BEDDINGTON

After our walk through the Lost Woods, Jane would often text me in the middle of the night. It was a collection of random thoughts, musings at an hour when most of the world slept, the texts somehow forming a tapestry of Jane.

Jane: 12:23 a.m.: *Doesn't this goat look just like a cow?*

Me: 12:25 a.m.: *Sorta. Why are you looking at pictures of goats in the middle of the night?*

Jane: 12:26 a.m.: *The better question is, why aren't you?*

Jane: 1:32 a.m.: *I think I want to go to clown college.*

Jane: 1:33 a.m.: *Not to be a clown, just to say I went to clown college.*

Jane: 1:45 a.m.: *I guess you don't care about my dreams.*

Jane: 1:53 a.m.: *I WON'T be performing at your birthday.*

One night, Jane texted me twenty-two times, ranging from the somewhat disconcerting *You look so peaceful while you sleep*, to articles about Bigfoot, the Yeti, and aliens disguised as our most celebrated politicians. I didn't see the texts until the next morning. When I saw her in biology, she looked withdrawn, safe behind her hoodie, her eyes half-closed.

"I couldn't sleep," she said.

"I know," I said, scanning through the texts, the last one a link to an article claiming the Bermuda Triangle was a front for government regulated alien abductions. "Is everything okay?"

Jane shrugged. "Sometimes my brain won't shut up." She looked down at her desk, tracing lines in her notebook.

Mr. Parker stood at the board in front of a picture of Aquaman. "He'd be classified as what type of species?"

"Hey," I whispered to Jane, "Aquaman working as a disgruntled barista who secretly dreams of becoming a Shakespearian actor."

Jane smirked. "That's a whole movie."

"But seriously, you know you can tell me stuff, right?"

She stopped doodling in her notebook and looked at me. "I like being distracted," she said. "Even if it's by men making coffee in Speedos."

"You mean, especially by men making coffee in Speedos."

Next class, Jane gave me a CD with all of Grandma Irene's greatest hits. "You have some homework," she whispered. Strangely enough, Mr. Parker's lesson that day had nothing to do with comic books, but instead consisted of reading from an old worn-out textbook. His schedule of comic book conventions was wearing on him.

I opened the CD case. Inside, Jane had drawn a picture of her grandmother playing guitar. There was a rainbow in the background, shining over a town that looked a lot like Burgerville, recognizable mostly from the random green cows dotting the land-scape. Jane had listed the tracks on the CD in black marker, titles like "Firsts" and "Tree Song" and "Freedom Strings."

"You're now ready to experience the awesomeness that was my grandmother," Jane said. "Her music always puts me in a good mood."

"I'm honored," I said.

As soon as I got home from school, I put the CD in my old stereo. Acoustic guitar filled the room as Grandma Irene sang about being happy, loving your neighbor, protesting injustice, and on one song, the miracle of peanut butter. I found myself tapping my foot and nodding my head to the music.

I wondered how Jane's grandmother could have been so happy. I mean, peanut butter's good, but is it that good? I also didn't understand how someone so happy could have become the sullen woman in the portrait hanging in the Does' stairwell. It somehow added a tinge of sadness to her music. There's a reason historians don't write about an event until after it's already over. The ending changes how you see the beginning and middle.

By the time winter break came around, Simon and I were con-fronted with the most shocking development in the history of Burgerville to date. Our friendship with Jane had earned us an invitation to the biggest party of the year, a rager at none other than Tommy Beddington's house.

On the night of the party, the three of us met at my house to get ready. Simon had on a Santa hat and a T-shirt featuring Santa Claus with his reindeer. Because Simon had bought it from his favorite custom T-shirt website, he appeared to be riding shotgun with Kris Kringle. Jane had dressed pretty much the same way she always did, with the exception of a red-and-green folk T-shirt that featured a bearded man who looked a lot like Santa Claus beneath the caption: *O Come, All Ye Folkful.* I'd decided to wear a green elf's hat and a hideous Christmas sweater, red and green wool knitted in uneven stripes, as if somebody was going blind when they made it.

"Who's driving?" I asked.

"Mom let me have the Red Rocket," Simon said, proud of the new moniker he had for his mom's minivan, and doubly proud that the inspiration came from a dog's erection.

"I call backseat," Jane said.

"But *I* wanted the backseat," I said.

The backseat gave you the best view of the sky; you could recline to an almost horizontal position and stare at the stars through the moon roof. It made you feel like you were in a rocket ship cruising through space.

"We can both sit in the back," Jane said.

"I'm not gonna be your chauffeur," Simon said.

"You can wear the hat." Jane pulled out an old World War II captain's hat I had in my room.

Simon paused and examined the hat, weighing his options.

"And you guys will call me Captain?"

"Sure," Jane said.

"Get us there safely, Captain," I added.

Simon seemed satisfied with the trade-off.

The Beddington family was still riding the coattails of the late, great Earl Beddington. After Earl passed away, his widow did her best to revive her husband's reputation. That's when they built the statue and toned down all the business about the green mutant cows.

Tommy Beddington's father, Thomas Beddington, on the other hand, did his best to ruin the family name. Apparently, he had taken the family's cow vendetta seriously and opened up a leather factory with the sole goal of killing as many cows as possible. Everyone knew he operated on the edge of the law, using his leather business as a front to embezzle money and other nefarious activities. People said he had connections with the mob and it was grudgingly accepted you couldn't become mayor of Burgerville unless he gave you his blessing—and the money to buy the election.

On the way to the party, Jane and I sat in the backseat of Simon's van, staring up at the stars. As Simon drove slowly through the winding streets of backcountry Burgerville, it felt like he had turned off his engine and was letting the gravitational pull of the party bring us closer. Directly overhead, the stars shone brighter than I'd ever seen them before. For a minute, it felt like we were getting closer to them, the Red Rocket taking off and leaving the atmosphere.

"Do you think Mr. Beddington really sold missile secrets to the Soviets?" Simon asked as we drove.

"Highly doubtful," I said.

"Do you think he dumped all that toxic waste in the river on purpose?" he asked, referring to a recent scandal involving the leather factory.

"Probably," I said.

"If you guys hate the Beddingtons so much, why are you going to their house?" Jane asked.

"Because," Simon said, thinking it unnecessary to finish his sentence.

"It's a rite of passage," I said. "And this is the first year we made the guest list."

"We weren't even invited to his laser tag party in the sixth grade," Simon said. "And that means even his parents didn't think we were cool."

"Their loss," Jane said. "Because I think you guys are the best thing about this town."

"You do?" Simon said, as if Jane had just admitted to chewing gum found in the water fountain.

"I do."

I waited for her to make a sarcastic comment, but she let the words hang in the air, a declarative statement.

I remained staring at the moon roof, afraid to speak; I was worried I'd get choked up. The fact that Jane had embraced Simon and me felt like a minor miracle.

"Now's our chance to show them just how fun we really are," Simon said. But his tone made it sound like a threat.

"Light speed, Captain," I said.

Simon pressed down on the gas pedal. The Red Rocket hummed loudly, rumbling and hissing as it accelerated.

By the time we arrived at the Beddington Estate, the party was in full swing: cars parked on the lawn, people milling around the grass like zombies, a steady bass creating an ominous pulse in the cold winter air.

Simon parked at the edge of the lawn. It felt like the Red Rocket had transported us to another planet. The three of us disembarked from the van, uncertainly stepping on the grass, as if we half expected the lack of gravity to bounce us back in the air.

Mary Reyes, a girl from my history class the previous year, saw us arrive and hobbled over, stumbling over a light fixture as she moved toward us. Before Jane arrived, Mary was the mysterious new girl, partly because she had moved from China, but mostly because the Burgerville rumor mill couldn't come to terms with all of her supposed contradictions. She looked Asian but her last name sounded Hispanic; she had lived in China but was spotted in Mr. Olsen's Chinese I class, which according to legend, Mr. Olsen couldn't pass himself.

The truth is, Mary isn't Chinese or Hispanic. She's Filipina. And she only lived in China for a year because her dad had been transferred there for work, after living in New Jersey her entire life. Just like when Jane first moved to Burgerville, the myth could trump the reality.

Mary's hair was tangled over her eyes, and she had on a pair of reindeer antlers, with her nose painted black.

"You three," she mumbled, almost accusingly.

"Hi, Mary," I said.

"Hi, Ray." We glanced toward the house and I knew we were thinking the same thing. How'd we both earn invites to Bedding-ton's party? A light snow began to fall, the sky losing its clarity, becoming glazed over in a powdery fog.

"It's like being in a snow globe," Simon said.

Jane had already begun walking to the party. She turned back to face us. The light from the house highlighted the snowflakes, and I watched them dance around Jane's head.

"What are you guys waiting for?" she asked.

"On, Comet," Simon said to Mary. She looked at him strangely, then led us to the house, staggering over the walkway in the most un-reindeer-like way possible. As she walked in front of us, I saw she also had a tail protruding from the top of her pants.

"She kind of reminds me of Rudolph's mom," Simon said, pointing at Mary. "How hot was *she*?"

Inside the house, the pulsating bass became a steady pounding, a heart on the verge of exploding.

The first thing I noticed about the house was the endless array of photographs of Tommy Beddington's father with influential people. From a collection of celebrities at the top to Burgerville councilmen at the bottom, the elder Beddington clearly wanted visitors to know what type of man he was.

"Holy shit," Simon said, pointing to a picture of Mr. Beddington with a celebrity I vaguely knew. "We're among royalty."

Jane walked along the wall and scanned the pictures. "*After* a revolution," Jane said. "These guys have all been dethroned."

I took a step back from the wall. It clearly wasn't a who's who, but a who *was,* an homage to the B list: Mr. T giving a thumbs-up to the camera; the Karate Kid posed in a fighting stance; the entire cast of *The Wonder Years*. It had a sinister quality, as if a picture on the wall was the way Mr. Beddington stole a person's energy and sapped their youth in order to stay young himself.

"Thirsty?" Jane asked, turning to me.

I nodded. "And a little hungry. Do you think they'll serve appetizers?"

Jane rolled her eyes.

We pushed our way through a crowd of people at the stairwell and walked to the kitchen, a shiny aluminum room. We found the keg lying in a bucket next to the fridge. Jane grabbed cups and pumped us each a beer.

Simon opened the fridge and took out a carton of milk. "I'm still growing," he said as he poured his milk into a red Solo cup.

It sounds weird, but it felt like the three of us existed in our own atmosphere. When we left the kitchen, the people realigned and we found ourselves in our own orbit, watching everyone float around us, untethered, lost in space as we held on to each other. The beer gave the scene a warm glow, as if I were watching from space as humanity tortured itself.

Jane leaned into me, a mysterious form of gravity pulling her closer. People were dancing, yelling, moving from room to room—chaos and entropy, the laws of the universe on full display.

"An authentic house party," Jane said. "I am now an official resident of the suburbs."

"I miss the old days," Simon said. "When parties meant an arts-and-crafts activity or rolling around in a ball pit."

"They still have those," I said. "And your birthday *is* coming up."

Jane held up her hand for silence and pointed to a couple across the room. They were making out, their faces stuck together.

When they unspooled, Simon looked disappointed. "She's in my English class," he said. "I thought she liked me."

"I don't think she's right for you," Jane said.

Simon took a sip of his milk. "That's what Mom said."

"You should probably stop discussing your love life with your mom," Jane said.

"Mom said that too," Simon said.

"Ray and I will take charge of finding you a girlfriend."

"A real one?" Simon asked.

"A real one," Jane repeated.

We all scanned the party, the who's who of Burgerville High packed closely together.

"Did I ever tell you guys about how Burgerville became Williamsburg?"

"Yes!" Simon and Jane both shouted together.

"No?" I said, ignoring them. "Well, it all started back in the 1950s when Burgerville was becoming the next big suburban metropolis."

Jane pretended to snore. Simon slapped himself in the face in an attempt to stay awake.

"Historians are always underappreciated in their time," I said.

"That's why we have historians," Jane said. "To tell us how important historians are."

As the music grew louder, the living room became even more densely packed. A sweaty jumble of people moving and swaying to the beat.

Jane scowled at the scene in front of her. People making out. Red Solo cups, overfilled, spilling beer onto the carpet. A coffee table was on its side, set up as a barricade, as a group of kids launched snowballs at unsuspecting victims. One of the popular girls, Laura Russell, stood in a small clique, taking video clips of the party to upload to social media, fragments of memories that would now forever exist in cyberspace—much to the embarrassment of Burgerville's future doctors, lawyers, and politicians.

Sufficiently annoyed, Jane turned her back to the party.

"Not what you had in mind when you moved to Burgerville?" I asked.

"Exactly what I had in mind."

"You should invite your friends from the city. Didn't you say Ellie was going to come out one of these days?"

Jane looked away. "She wanted to come tonight, but there was a sighting of the Yeti in Upstate New York. Ellie's there now, hoping to be the first woman to photograph it."

I could have called her on it, but I didn't. I figured she was still not sure whether there was a way for her two lives to coexist. I played along.

"You're saying someone's already caught the Yeti on film?"

"Of course," Jane said. "Don't you pay attention to the news?"

"I guess I missed it . . . Maybe when Ellie comes back, then."

"Maybe," Jane said.

She drank, practically tipped the cup upside down to get every last bit, then said, "I'm thirsty again." She held the cup between her teeth, raised her eyebrows, and disappeared into the crowd, not bothering to ask me if I wanted a refill too.

"I think she's upset," I said to Simon.

"It's probably something you said." Simon crossed his legs the way kids do when they have to go to the bathroom. "I really have to pee."

"Good talk," I said.

"I wasn't saying it's your fault, just that you might have hit a sensitive spot by accident and I just drank a lot of milk, so if I don't go to the bathroom right now I'll be the only non-drunk person to ever pee their pants at a party."

With that, Simon went off to find a bathroom.

I had gotten so used to traveling as a pack that being cast out on my own felt like cruel and unusual punishment. I was someone with Simon and Jane; out here in the wild, I was the same person I'd always been: Raymond Green, the quiet kid your parents made you invite to your birthday party.

I made my way to the kitchen, hoping to get another cup of beer and find Jane. When I got close to the keg, I saw her standing with Tommy Beddington, deep in conversation. The party pressed in on them, forcing them closer. Jane threw her head back in laughter and tapped his arm. Good one, Beddington! In that moment, he became one of the worst people in the world to me, in the same company as Genghis Khan and the guy who invented the Snuggie.

I marched toward the keg, doing everything in my power to convey dominance, short of beating my chest and throwing feces. The beer added a layer of drama to my movements. My shadow cast over the keg: foreboding. My glassy-eyed stare at Tommy: chilling. My slow and lumbered reach for the keg pump: orchestra crescendo! I took my cup and started pumping the keg, all the while watching Jane and Tommy engage in what I assumed to be some sort of mating ritual. I lost myself in the up-and-down motion of the pump, so much so that when I went to fill my cup, the beer sprayed all over the room. The people around me yelled out like monkeys chattering before a fight. My body went completely rigid. Part of me felt that if I stayed still maybe I could disappear. But of course, instead of disappearing, I just looked guilty. Tommy came over with a towel and began wiping up the beer. He took the spigot out of my hand as if he were my dad, punishing me by taking away my favorite toy.

"Only a couple of pumps," he said, "or else the beer goes everywhere."

I wanted to take the spigot and shove it right in Tommy Beddington's mouth. Instead, I nodded, said my *mea culpas*, and put out my cup like a child asking for more juice.

Then Jane walked over.

"You know Ray, right?" Jane asked as she put her cup under the spigot for a refill.

"We go way back," Beddington said. I snorted, a laugh caught too late. I wasn't going to be a pawn in Beddington's game.

I cleared my throat, attempting to recover from my laugh. "We're part of the lifers."

Jane and Beddington looked at me blankly.

"People who've lived in Burgerville their whole life. It's funny 'cause it's also the term they use for prison."

Classic Jane humor, but she didn't budge, almost seemed embarrassed by me.

"How do you guys know each other?" I asked.

"We have gym together," Jane said.

I thought of Jane wearing tight shorts and a tank top and became even more jealous.

"Gym!" I said loudly, sounding as if I'd solved a mystery. AHA!

"We're on the same badminton team," Tommy said. "Undefeated for the last three classes." He put his hand up and Jane high-fived him. The only logical explanation, I concluded, was that Jane had been possessed by a demon who loved team sports.

"Anyway, we're gonna go on a tour of the house," Tommy said to me. He gave me a look, the one guys give when they're practicing some sort of code. Unfortunately for him, no one had ever bothered to teach it to me.

"Cool," I said. "Let's go." I refilled my beer with two gentle pumps—high on the moment, I think I may have even winked at Tommy—and followed them.

"We've owned this land for over a hundred years," Tommy said, holding a door open for Jane and me.

The door opened to a room full of deer heads, a bear, something with tusks, and antique guns scattered throughout, as if the designer had tried to match the animal with their instrument of death.

Jane walked right up to one of the deer, touched its antlers, and stood in front of it, almost eye-to-eye.

"It's like he's looking back at me."

"My grandfather loved to hunt," Beddington said.

He also thought a group of mutant cows invaded the town, I added to myself.

"This way," Tommy said, motioning to yet another door. "Ladies first," he added as he waited for Jane and me to pass through the doorway.

The next room was full of people packed together from wall to wall. I saw Simon in the crowd, examining the party like a scientist studying a new species.

"Simon!" I yelled.

His head jerked, trying to find the source of his name. He was standing under a gigantic family portrait of the Beddingtons that looked like it had been lifted from a clothing catalogue. They were all in front of a lighthouse, wearing matching outfits, with draped sweaters over their shoulders. They smiled the kind of phony grin a kindergartner might draw on a stick figure. Not pictured: the toxic waste from the leather factory or enforcers from the mob.

Simon scanned the crowd, finally stopping when he got to me. He pointed at the portrait and started laughing. I pointed to the real-life Tommy to my right, who wasn't enjoying the joke nearly as much.

Simon's face turned red.

"My parents made me do it," Tommy said to me.

"You all look very . . . warm," I said, referring to the sweaters.

By the time Simon made it over to us, Tommy had wandered away to clean puke off his parents' carpet. Apparently, a drinking game involving *How the Grinch Stole Christmas* had gotten a little out of hand.

"So that was awkward," Simon said. "Why were you standing next to Tommy Beddington, anyway?"

"I don't know," I said, still attempting to uncover the truth behind Jane's friendship with him.

Jane stayed silent. She sighed and rolled her eyes.

"What's with *her*?" Simon asked.

"You'll have to ask her."

"*She's* right here," Jane said.

"When'd you become friends with Tommy Beddington?" I asked.

"I don't know."

"You know he's the devil incarnate, right?" Simon said. "You know about the pudding incident, don't you?"

"That was two years ago. He's actually a really nice guy."

"If you mean in the sense that Attila the Hun wasn't so bad once you got to know him, or Vlad the Impaler was just misunderstood, then yeah, great guy." Sometimes I could use my powers of history against people.

"We're at his house," Jane said.

"That's what people do in high school," I said. "They use people when it's convenient for them. You do it too."

"What's that supposed to mean?" Jane said.

Someone dressed as Santa walked by and started dancing near Jane. Jane stood still, ignoring the odd spectacle.

"Now that you're friends with Tommy Beddington, how much longer are you gonna hang out with Simon and me?"

Jane's face went flush.

A pause in the music. I felt my mouth go dry and the fogginess from the beer dissipate. Why did I say that?

This is one of the memories that kills me the most when I think about Jane. In the grand scheme of things it wasn't a big deal, but when I saw her face, I wanted to curl up in a ball and disappear.

"Santa Claus and Mrs. Claus having sex," I said, hoping to distract Jane from my stupidity with another random image.

She stormed off, leaving Simon, Santa, and me completely alone.

"I know what Santa wants for Christmas," Santa said.

"No one asked you," I said.

It wasn't until a couple of hours later that I saw Jane again. Simon and I were holed up in a corner watching everything built up in the previous few hours implode. The keg went dry. The energetic dancing degenerated into a scene from *The Night of the Living Dead,* accompanied by the weakening pulse of the music. It felt like we had entered a sort of Twilight Zone, where the longer we stayed, the more difficult it became to leave.

"You shouldn't have said that," Simon said.

The scene played on a loop in my head, reaching its inevitable conclusion again and again—time travel without the benefit of changing the past. "You're not helping," I said. "It's not like I killed her firstborn child."

"When you apologize, I'd lead with that," Simon said.

I downed the last of my beer. "I'm going to find Jane."

I zigzagged through the crowd, the party slowed to a crawl. It reminded me of one of those nature shows that uses a slow-motion camera to capture the inner workings of something we take for granted, like a bee pollinating a flower or a spider capturing its prey. Up close, it was horrifying.

I walked through the hunting room, into the shiny kitchen, back to the wall of B-list celebrities, but still couldn't find her. A feeling of dread hit my stomach. Could she be with Tommy?

The long and winding staircase beckoned me. Somehow I knew I had to confront whatever lay beyond those stairs. Floating outside of myself again, I watched from above as I ascended the steps, ready to confront Beddington if I had to, a hero on his way to slay the dragon. I thought it might be my last chance to tell Jane how I really felt.

By the time I reached the upstairs, I discovered another obstacle: a long hallway of closed doors. I slowly marched through the gauntlet, on the lookout for any sign of Jane. Then I saw it. All the way at the end, a door with a sports banner and yellow caution tape strewn across. It had to be Beddington's room.

It became clear to me what I had to do. I walked toward the door and knocked as loud as I could.

"Go away," Tommy Beddington's voice thundered through.

"Not until I talk to Jane!" I yelled back.

I jiggled the doorknob and rammed my shoulder into the door. I felt the old lock give as the casing on the door cracked. I had become a one-man demolition team.

The room flooded with light from the hallway. Beddington sprang out of bed in a fighting stance as his covers flipped back, concealing the person underneath.

"What the fuck, Ray?" Beddington said.

Something about the light and Beddington in his boxers—posed in a boxer's stance—made me reevaluate my original plan. My anger at Beddington dissolved into sadness. The confrontation felt like a punishment.

I backed out of the room slowly.

"Sorry," I mumbled to Beddington. "Jane," I said, addressing the figure under the blanket, "I just wanted to say I'm sorry."

I heard Jane's voice, loud and clear.

"Sorry for what?" she said from the hallway behind me.

I turned around. Jane stood there, a confused expression on her face.

"Then who's . . .?"

The covers flipped back. Steven Peters from the choir, shirtless, hair in all directions, squinted into the light. "Is that you, Ray?"

Beddington took a seat on the bed, glancing back and forth at Jane and me. He had this look on his face, like he was scared, angry, and confused all at the same time. I don't think I'd ever felt like such an asshole in my entire life.

"You won't tell anyone, right?" Beddington said.

"No," I said, my adrenaline dissipating. "Sorry about your door," I added.

"Just get out!" Tommy yelled. I closed the door behind me as best I could and came face-to-face with Jane.

"What the hell was that all about?" she asked, an edge to her voice.

"I . . . uh . . ." I couldn't quite put my thoughts into words. My buzz had worn off the second I walked into Beddington's room.

"You can't just go barging in on people," she said. She began to walk away from me. I followed her down the stairs, out the front door, and into the cold.

"I'm sorry," I called after her.

Jane stopped in the middle of the lawn. She had her back to me. It was snowing a lot harder than it was when we first got there.

"I'm sorry about what I said before."

"Is that what you think of me?" she said. "That I would use you to get to Beddington?"

"I don't know what I was thinking."

"I can't believe you'd act like such a jerk. You owe Tommy an apology."

"I know. It's just that . . ." I searched for the right thing to say. "You know how Grandma Irene's music always puts you in a good mood? That's how I feel about you. When you're around, I'm just happy. I guess I was scared I'd lose you, that you'd want to be with someone like him instead of someone like me."

Jane turned around to face me. She shook her head. "You're really smart about history, but you can be a real idiot when it comes to what's going on right in front of your face."

I looked away. I figured I blew it.

It seemed like she was about to say something else, but instead, she walked over to the Red Rocket and opened the back door. "No one locks their car in the suburbs," she said. She got in and sat down. Reclined so far back, she was almost completely horizontal. "Are you coming?" she said.

"Should I get Simon?"

"Not yet," she said.

I gulped, not sure if she was about to kill me or kiss me. But nothing was going to stop me from finding out which. I joined her in the van and tilted my seat to be even with hers. It felt like we were lying down in bed together. Snow was collecting on the roof, but I could still make out the clouds moving across the sky, the moon lighting up the edges. I slid the door shut.

"How would you tell our story?" Jane asked.

"Our story's not over," I said. "At least I hope it's not. Historians need perspective."

"But if you had to . . ."

I took a deep breath and exhaled. A cloud of vapor swirled around me. "I'd talk about the joke you made on your first day in Mr. Parker's class. About the presidents on Mount Rushmore. How that's when I knew how funny you are."

"What else?"

"The night you came over to my house and we played Never Have I Ever. How you covered your eyes during *The Butcher*." I smiled just thinking about it. "You let your guard down. And I knew I'd fight the Butcher to protect you, even if it meant ending up in one of his soups."

Jane laughed. "Keep going."

"I don't know, all the little moments. The times I realized how much there was to you . . . to us." I glanced at her. It was the first time I'd ever spoken about us as an *us*. She was looking up at the sky, but I could tell she was smiling. "Roger Lutz says the problem with studying history is that there's too much of it. That's how I feel about you."

"That there's too much of me? You were doing so well . . ."

"That didn't come out right. I mean there's too many great moments to choose from."

"Better." She scooched off her seat and made her way toward me. "Is there room for me?" she said. I tried to speak, but no sound came out. She sat on my lap and wrapped her arms around me. Our breath mixed into a single cloud. The snow continued to collect on the roof; it felt like the world was burying us in this moment. Jane leaned forward and her hair brushed against my face. Then she kissed me, and I couldn't help but think that I had just been wandering around trying to make my way to this.

When she pulled back, her eyes were still closed.

I thought back to our pact about telling each other when and if our wishes came true. "Delaney's one for three," I said.

"You mean?"

I nodded.

Before I could say anything else, she leaned forward once again.

We kept kissing until the lights in the van turned on and we heard a knock from outside. Simon stood there, a look of disappointment on his face.

"Sorry," Jane and I said together, sitting up. Simon nonchalantly got in the front seat and closed the door.

"It was unlocked," I said.

"Am I just a chauffeur to you now?"

"*The* chauffer," Jane said.

"I'm supposed to be the first one to make out in my mom's minivan," he said with a sigh. Then he started the Red Rocket and we headed home.

208 DAYS AFTER

MAKE-BELIEVE

It's Christmas Eve. I can't believe it's been over a year since that night at Beddington's.

I can hear my mom and Tim downstairs, decorating the Christmas tree. At first, my mom tried to keep our life separate from her relationship with Tim, but now it feels like we took in a stray dog who won't leave us alone. Tim's been coming over more and more. Eating dinner, watching TV, checking up on me if my mom has to work late. Tim the superhero, the rescuer, or even worse, the role model, as my mom once called him.

"Ray," she yells up the stairs, "we're about to light the Christmas tree."

"I'll be right down," I say, with no intention of actually leaving my room. Then the scent of cookies wafts into my bedroom from the vent that connects to the kitchen, and I immediately change my mind.

"Hey, Bud," Tim says when I walk down the stairs. Tim's new nickname for me. I am now a *Bud*.

"What do you say, Ray?" my mom says as if I'm a five-year-old learning to say *please* and *thank you*.

"Hi, Tim."

My mom looks back and forth at Tim and me, waiting for a conversation to begin.

"It's been cold," I say. Rich would at least want me to try.

Tim nods. "The weatherman says we're due for more snow."

Fascinating, I think. Somebody please write this conversation down. This must be preserved for future generations!

"What's Simon up to?" my mom asks after realizing the conversation has reached its disappointing crescendo.

"I don't know." It's true. We've been hanging out less and less. We didn't have a big fight or anything, just a bunch of little steps away from each other. "Where are the cookies?"

"In the kitchen. But first you're gonna watch the tree light up."

"Now I'm being ordered to participate in Christmas?"

She plugs in the lights. Only a few of the bulbs come to life. Brand-new ornaments are hung around the tree, all the references to my dad mysteriously missing.

The star shines brightly, then makes a buzzing noise and goes out.

"Well, that was anticlimactic," I say.

Tim turns off the lamp in the family room, letting the few bulbs that work paint the room in a dim rainbow. "It's just enough," he says.

Out of the corner of my eye, I see my mom reach out and touch his hand. Regardless of how I feel about it, my mom is happy.

"Can I go now?" I ask.

"I know it's early," Tim says, "but . . ."

He grabs a wrapped present from under the tree.

I think he expects me to open it, but I don't have it in me to rip off the paper like a little kid, and say thanks to the camera and how it's exactly what I wanted.

"Did you get a gift for Tim from me?" I ask my mom.

Tim laughs. "No gift necessary."

The altruistic bastard.

With nothing else to say, I walk back up the stairs, using Tim's present as a tray for my milk and cookies, and after the gift has served its purpose, I throw it in the trash unopened. I don't want another piece of sports memorabilia. I don't want anything. For a moment, I feel guilty. I owe it to my mom to get along with Tim, to accept his presents and be one of those perfect kids who call pretty much anyone who can play catch Dad.

But I'm not. I walk back to the garbage can and step on the present, pushing it to the bottom with all of my weight. I hear the sound of glass breaking, and it feels good, this small act of destruction, tapping into my anger while the rest of the world is singing songs and spreading holiday cheer. I peer into the garbage can and see the jagged fragments of Tim's gift: a framed photo of Jane and me making grotesque faces at the camera. An inevitable result of my mom telling us to smile.

I glance down at the frame in the garbage can and see an inscription: *History is the one thing that can neither be created nor destroyed.* I know Tim means well. I know everyone means well. But all the platitudes and words of wisdom and therapy exercises don't actually change anything. And the only appropriate reaction I can think of is to break stuff.

I imagine all the kids who believe in Santa and a benevolent universe that keeps score, rewarding the good and punishing the bad.

But I don't believe that anymore. Now I don't know what I believe.

167–133 DAYS BEFORE

WHEN SIMON MET MARY

After our kiss at Beddington's Christmas party, Jane and I settled into our new relationship status, gradually building our own history onto the history of Burgerville. We became boyfriend and girlfriend when I accidentally gave us the labels in a text. We were joking around, thinking of ways to freak out Simon when school started again.

Jane: 5:45 p.m.: *Matching outfits.*

Me: 5:46 p.m.: *Fake tattoos with each other's initials.*

Jane: 5:47 p.m.: *Going to school on one of those bikes with two seats. What are they called?*

Me: 5:47 p.m.: *Not sure. I've never had a girlfriend before. And Simon would always say he was busy when I asked him to rent one with me . . .*

Jane: 5:47 p.m.: *Are you calling me your girlfriend?*

I almost threw my phone against the wall. What was I thinking? I kept trying to come up with a cool response, but nothing sounded right. I even texted Simon for help, but I'm pretty sure he was in his vampire book club at the time, because all he texted back was a customized vampire emoji. I knew I didn't have much time, so I tried to act like it was no big deal.

Me: 5:51 p.m.: *If I was, would that be okay?*

It felt like hours before Jane texted me back. I imagined her trying to let me off easy. Or maybe she would just never talk to me again. Then I realized only thirty seconds had passed.

Jane: 5:52 p.m.: *Yes, boyfriend.*

The next day in class, Jane presented me with a detailed list of relationship rules. "Sometimes I need space. No hand-holding in public. No cute animal nicknames. And lastly, but most importantly, please don't ever smell my hair."

"But I like smelling your hair," I said.

"I'll think about it," she said, smiling at me.

"It's very normal," Mr. Parker said, suddenly appearing in front of our desks. "Hair secretes a natural pheromone designed to attract potential mates. That's why I love the comic book . . ."

Mr. Parker finished an explanation that had something to do with the Tick, though he seemed to confuse himself mid-sentence: "Or am I thinking about Mantis from *The Avengers*?" Luckily, I remembered to close my notebook so Mr. Parker couldn't see the picture Jane had drawn of him dressed as Batman eating a burrito. That'd be an awkward conversation.

Jane and I were also making out whenever we got the chance, though the conditions weren't always ideal. We'd either have to awkwardly position ourselves in the car, withstand frigid temperatures in the Lost Woods, or keep an eye out for Mrs. Doe, who seemed obsessed with getting us snacks and knowing whether or not we'd read about the most recent bear sightings in the *Burgerville Gazette*.

Still, I could tell Jane was struggling with something she wasn't ready to share with me. She seemed to barely sleep, texting me at all hours of the night, bags under her eyes the next day, the occasional nap during Mr. Parker's lectures. She'd also sometimes be in a bad mood for no apparent reason. When I'd ask what was bothering her, she'd say things like "Global warming" or "Pineapple Melody just broke up" or "People who make their dogs dress as the mailman for Halloween."

I worried I'd push her away by asking too many questions, so instead, I did my best to cheer her up with my random image technique. For example, her comment about dogs dressed up as mailmen pretty much wrote itself: "Hey," I said to her that day. "Think about . . . wait, this just came to me . . . a dog dressed up as a mailman." She didn't react, so I took it up a notch. "And he's being barked at by a man dressed as a dog."

Jane cracked a smile.

A little while after Christmas vacation ended, I sought Tommy Beddington out to apologize for barging in on him at the party. I wasn't sure exactly what to say. How much he even wanted me to say. I found him in the library, wearing his letterman jacket as always, sitting at a desk near a window. He was looking out at the parking lot, listening to music.

"Hey, Tommy," I said.

He took his headphones off. "Hey, Ray." He was filling out a worksheet about the French Revolution. His class was still right at the beginning, when things looked all rosy and full of hope. "I hope you like severed heads," I said.

"What?"

I realized that probably wasn't the most normal thing to say. "The French Revolution," I said. "Things are about to get very bloody."

"Can't wait," Tommy said.

A pause. My mind went blank. The fluorescent lights seemed brighter than usual. The clacking of computer keys. The low mumble of voices as kids traded homework, discussed math problems, brainstormed swear words to write on the tables. I had to say something.

"I'm sorry about—"

He waved me off. "We're good."

I realized Steven was sitting a few tables away. He glanced over at us, then quickly looked back down at his book. I could tell Beddington was getting nervous, as if I might betray him through a look or accidentally saying the wrong thing.

"It was a great party," I said. "And I would know a thing or two about parties."

He gave me a look like, *Is there anything else I can help you with?* It felt like a glimmer of the old Tommy Beddington had returned.

"We should all hang out sometime," I said, just trying to fill the empty space and leave on a positive note. People spend so much time talking about how to start conversations, they forget to teach you how to end them.

"Yeah, whatever," he said. I followed his gaze back to Steven. I wondered what it must have been like for him. To be cloaked in a letterman jacket, surrounded by his football friends, just out of reach from what he really wanted.

"If you need any help with the French Revolution, just let me know. I'm full of fun facts about the guillotine."

Beddington smiled. "I'll keep that in mind."

While I was enjoying all the benefits that went along with having a girlfriend, Simon seemed to be having a difficult time adjusting to

Jane and me being a couple. "But what happens if you guys break up?" he asked us.

"I'll get full custody," I told him.

"How will I know when I'm the third wheel?"

"We'll tell you," Jane said.

"You mean like a signal?"

"Kind of," Jane said, "except instead of a signal I'll tell you."

Jane renewed her search to find Simon a girlfriend to help him adjust.

"What's your type?" Jane asked him.

"She has to be female," he said.

"Could you give me a bit more detail?"

"I think medium is a good starting point," he said.

"It's not a soft drink size," I said.

"Now you're the expert on women?"

"I do have a girlfriend."

"Yeah, but Jane doesn't count."

"What's that supposed to mean?" Jane said.

"You're like our sister."

Jane rolled her eyes.

"Let's find a medium girl," I said, realizing the only way to approach this was through the lens of Simon and that he was really just talking about the Goldilocks Principle in his own Simon way: He wanted someone who was *just right*.

Our search ended when, soon after our conversation, Jane suggested Mary Reyes, the reindeer from Beddington's Christmas party.

"Why Mary?" I asked.

"Well, at Beddington's party, we talked for a bit. She told me all about her dogs, the play she was working on . . . Then she asked about Simon. You know, all like, *What's his story?* and that kind of stuff. I thought she was asking because she figured something was wrong with him, but now I'm thinking it was because she liked him."

"But is she medium enough?"

"I guess we'll have to wait and see."

At first, Simon was a little hesitant when Jane and I told him about Mary.

"Mary Reyes?" Simon said. "Doesn't she occasionally dress up as Lady Macbeth?"

"Yes, but she was also Rudolph's mom," I reminded him, hoping to rekindle the attraction he felt when he'd seen her wearing antlers. "Plus, she's still sort of new. It's only a matter of time before the jocks take notice."

Simon considered the proposition and then took a deep breath. "You're right, we better do it before she realizes she's out of my league," he said. "I'm in."

Mary suggested we meet at the combo burger/Chinese restaurant in town called O'Reilly's Pub and Grill, the perfect embodiment of America's melting pot and cultural appropriation, as the O'Reillys aren't American, Irish, or Chinese, but apparently Slovenian.

Jane and I arrived early so we could go over the game plan—topics to bring up, stories to avoid, a safe word to create a distraction if Simon needed help. The inside of the restaurant reflected the uncertainty of the owners. The dark atmosphere felt like an Irish pub, while the decorations looked like they had been assembled from tourist shops all around the world. A gold dragon sat at the front entrance, alongside a wooden sculpture of a leprechaun. A gigantic Buddha rested atop a full-size green cow, complete with removable body parts so you could see which part of the animal you were eating.

Jane scanned the surroundings, watching the waiters rush by, each wearing a different piece of wisdom on their shirt, all clearly lifted directly from fortune cookies: *If you have something good in your life, don't let it go! Our deeds determine us almost as much as we determine our deeds.*

"If you asked me last January where I'd be in a year, it wouldn't have been here," Jane said.

Part of me took it as an insult. The other part of me wanted to ask what year-ago Jane would have responded, although I knew I wouldn't get a straight answer. And truthfully, I didn't know if I wanted one.

Jane must have seen I was offended, because she put her hand on my arm and said, "But there's no place I'd rather be."

Then, as if she caught herself being too nice, quickly added, "Yuck. I sound like a Hallmark card."

"Everybody likes a Hallmark card," I said.

"I don't."

"You know you can be confusing sometimes?"

"That's a good thing, right?"

"It's a confusing thing," I said.

"It's just that I don't believe in big romantic gestures. *Huge* promises. All of the stuff you see in movies and TV shows."

"What do you believe in, then?"

"I don't know. I used to think that I needed to live some big, crazy, adventurous life. Ellie and I hanging out at folk clubs, chasing some ridiculous conspiracy theory. But now I think I just want *normal*."

"Then I'm your guy," I said.

Soon after, Simon walked in, wearing his tuxedo T-shirt with his hair gelled back.

"Really?" I said as he got closer to our table.

"What?"

"You look like you're wearing a Simon costume."

"It's not like the original's been working so well." Simon took a seat and put the napkin in his shirt like a bib; after Jane gave him a funny look, he laid it flat on his lap.

"Did she already back out?" he asked, nodding to the empty seat next to him.

"Her mom's dropping her off and you're giving her a ride back home," Jane said, winking.

"The Red Rocket's maiden voyage, if you know what I mean."

"You're hopeless," Jane said.

The heavy smell of fried food hung in the air, egg rolls mixing with french fries. Simon breathed in the air and closed his eyes as if meditating. After a few moments of quiet, he came out of his trance. Looking back and forth at Jane and me, he appeared to be on the verge of delivering a speech.

"Thanks, guys," he said.

Jane and I both nodded.

"We're go for liftoff."

Mary walked in soon after. She had also dressed up for the occasion, wearing a frilly dress that would have been more appropriate for a 1950s Sadie Hawkins dance.

Simon was evidently pleased, as he suddenly started sweating and saying random words, none of the sentences quite working together. It sounded like he was playing Scrabble and only had a few letters to choose from.

"I . . . Uh . . . Dinner . . . Fortune cookie . . ."

Mary looked to me for translation.

I shrugged.

But after he calmed down and had a chance to sit in silence and read the menu, Simon was able to collect himself and for better or worse, be Simon.

"I love Chinese food," he said soon after we had finished ordering. "Did I ever tell you guys that I used to write my own fortune cookie sayings?"

I shook my head, a cue for Simon to stop, but which he took as an invitation to continue.

"Yeah, I used to shove them in my mom's cookies with semi-motivational sayings like, *You're not as bad as everyone thinks* and *Set your sights lower. That way, even if you trip, it won't hurt that much.* One day, my dad choked on one of the cookies and my mom had to give him the Heimlich. But here's the weird part. Guess what fortune he choked on?"

Simon took a sip of water and waited, letting us know his question was not rhetorical.

"What fortune did he choke on?" I asked in order to hurry Simon along.

"It read, *Treat your life like you treat your food; don't choke and make sure it's full of flavor.*"

I looked nervously to Mary, worried she was already trying to figure out an escape plan. But instead she leaned forward and said, "That's so strange. I used to write my own horoscopes. But then they started to come true . . ."

An ominous silence settled over the table.

"I'm just kidding," Mary said, laughing. Then her smile disappeared. "Or am I?"

"Sounds like a horror movie," Simon said. "*Horrorscope: Scorpio's Revenge.*"

"*Horrorscope Two . . . Cancer,*" Mary shot back.

"She's funny," Jane whispered to me.

"I think we found Simon's soulmate," I whispered back.

By the time our food arrived, the conversation was humming along. That's when Jane decided to bring out the big guns.

"Simon's family is actually famous in town," she said.

"Really?" Mary asked, taking a bite out of her burger.

"For being failures," Simon said, chewing his food with his mouth open.

"But really successful failures," I said.

Hoping to give Simon another chance to shine, I tried to steer the conversation to his love of vampire fiction.

"Every time I go to the signings, it's like me and a bunch of twelve-year-old girls," he said.

Okay, in retrospect that probably wasn't the best topic to bring up. But Mary didn't seem to mind. In fact, she began listing the titles of her favorite vampire novels, an odd collection of books with names like *Fangtastic* and *Stake Through the Heart: A Vampire Love Story.*

After the vampire conversation died down, we shared our battle scars from Burgerville. "My first day here I went home and cried,"

Mary said. "It was like everyone had a different story about my life, all these crazy rumors about where I was from, why I was in Burgerville. I just wanted to disappear. If it weren't for a flyer to try out for *Macbeth* and join the theater department, I don't know how I would've survived."

"Who'd you end up playing?" Jane asked.

"I was Lady Macbeth's stunt double."

"That's awesome," Simon said.

"But I know exactly what you mean," Jane said. "Moving to Burgerville from Brooklyn felt like moving to a different country. I'd hear people whisper about me. All this made-up stuff about my life. Thank god I got rid of Facebook a long time ago."

"It's different when you grow up here," Simon said, slurping his milk. "Everything seems totally normal. You kind of forget another world exists."

"What do you think, Ray?" Jane asked. "Have you always been Mr. Burgerville?"

"I don't think I'd put it quite like that, but I've always loved the history," I said. "When I was younger, my dad would take me to all the weird places and tell me stories about the town. So I've always seen two Burgervilles."

I could feel Jane's eyes on me. The kind of gaze that makes you feel like someone's looking directly into your soul—or you have a piece of food in your teeth.

"You should really make a Burgerville pamphlet or something," Jane said. She playfully kicked my foot underneath the table.

"Wait," Simon said to Jane. "If Ray's Mr. Burgerville, doesn't that make you Mrs. Burgerville?"

Jane seemed to really consider this. She moved the food around her plate with the same focus she gave her drawings in biology. "I guess," she said, "but can I keep my own last name?"

By the end of the meal, Mary and Simon had inched closer to each other and their legs were touching. Simon smiled like a miracle was taking place.

The waiter brought over the check and laid out four fortune cookies in the center of the table.

Mary unwrapped the first cookie, broke it in half, and retrieved the little strip of paper from the center. She read it and smiled.

"What'd it say?" Simon asked.

She passed it to Simon. "*The one you love is closer than you think*," Simon read. Simon looked around the restaurant, now practically empty, then returned his attention to the table. "Do you know any of the busboys or waiters?"

"No," Mary said. "Why?"

"No reason," he said. Following Mary's lead, he unwrapped his cookie, but instead of breaking it apart, he went straight for a bite; the fortune hung out of his mouth as cookie crumbs fell onto the table.

"I got one of those motivational fortune cookies for depressed people," he said. He read from his fortune: "*You are pleasant to be around*."

"At least it's true," Mary said. Simon beamed like a kindergartner who had just received a gold star.

"Maybe there's something to this whole fortune cookie thing after all," I said. I cracked open my cookie: *Be on the lookout for coming events. They cast a shadow beforehand,* it read.

I ripped it in half and put it in a glass of water.

Simon looked at me funny. "What'd it say, Ray?"

"Nothing. What about yours, Jane?" I asked in an attempt to change the subject.

Jane took her fist and smashed it on the last remaining cookie. Shards of mutilated wafer showed through the flattened plastic.

"That's what I think of fortunes," Jane said. As we got up to leave, I pocketed the smashed cookie, curious to see for myself what was in store for Jane.

133 DAYS BEFORE, CONT'D

THE MCCALLEN MANSION

We left the restaurant and walked out into the cold air, shivering but feeling relief from the oppressive fried food miasma of O'Reilly's.

"I have an idea," Jane said as we stood in the parking lot. "Simon, you have the Red Rocket, right?"

Simon nodded.

"Great. Ray, flashlights?"

"Cellphone should do the trick."

"Mary, are you afraid of ghosts?"

"Only my grandmother's," Mary said. "She always said she was going to haunt me when she died."

"Wait," Simon said. "You can't mean—"

"The McCallen Mansion," I said solemnly. "It's been on the list for a few months. But tonight? Are you sure?"

"There's no time like the present," Jane said.

"What's the McCallen Mansion?" Mary asked.

"Only the most haunted house in Burgerville," I said.

"Of course Burgerville has a haunted house," Mary said.

"*The* haunted house," Jane said. "You probably don't know this, but Burgerville actually began as a hospital for the mentally ill. Back when Burgerville was just farmland, this guy A. J. McCallen came here from Ireland to start his utopia."

Jane smiled at me. She must have read Roger Lutz's book about the McCallen Mansion. "But they weren't attracting the most reputable settlers. Right, Ray?"

"Yup. Early Burgerville was populated mostly by criminals and vagrants."

"So McCallen had no choice but to open what's come to be known as the world's first humane asylum in order to treat all the—how can I put it nicely?—*interesting* people that settled here."

"Like my great-great-grandpa," Simon said.

"Okay," Mary said, sounding skeptical, "but what about his unfinished business? Why's he haunting the place?"

"Ray?"

"He . . ." I didn't want to say.

"Go ahead, Ray," Jane said.

"He killed himself. Right inside the mansion. He was so busy treating his patients, he never got the help he needed. Ever since then, there's been sightings of him wandering around the mansion, forever trying to cure Burgerville."

"He's got his work cut out for him," Jane said.

"You're not afraid, are you?" Jane asked Simon on the way over.

"No," Simon said, glancing at Mary. "Of course not."

"Good," Jane said. "Then you can go in first. Who knows what's in that house."

As we drove, we all sat in silence, the expansive night sky above our heads, stars hidden behind dark clouds. Jane and I reclined in the backseat, while Mary rode up front with Simon.

"It's supposed to snow," Simon said, sounding worried.

"If we get stranded, I call not being the first one eaten," Mary said.

"Damn it," Simon said. "Well played."

With that, as if to test our resolve, the first snowflake hit Simon's windshield. But McCallen must have been calling to us, because no one even suggested we turn around.

By the time we reached the house, a couple inches of snow had already piled up.

The headlights cast a spotlight on the dilapidated exterior of the house. The gray shingles were chipped in some places and completely gone in others. The windows on the top floor had been boarded up, which made it seem like the house had its eyes closed to the world. A plaque was placed next to the front door sometime in the 1970s that read: *The McCallen Mansion, Est. 1862*. It was too far away to read, but every true citizen of Burgerville knew the inscription by heart: *Give us your tired, your hungry, your mentally ill.*

Jane slid open the car door and stared at the imposing façade. I climbed out of the minivan and stood a few feet behind her; she looked tiny in front of the imposing structure of the mansion.

Simon got out of the car and, in a move that shocked both Jane and me, extended his hand to Mary. Together, they walked toward the house. Jane and I followed a few yards back, arms at our sides.

We crept quietly toward the front door. The wind picked up; snowflakes swirled wildly around our heads. When we reached the front steps, we stopped as if an invisible force field barred our entrance.

Jane lightly pushed Simon. "Good luck," she said.

"It was *your* idea."

"I'll do it," I said, feeling brave for no particular reason.

"I heard people come here to have sex," Simon said.

Mary looked frightened.

"Not us," Simon quickly added.

I walked to the front door, unsure what to expect. My mom had been warning me about the McCallen Mansion for years. The few times Simon and I had planned on going there, something in the news always kept us away. Like the time an escaped prisoner was found hiding there, or the bear that was discovered hibernating in the kitchen, or, of course, the continued rumors of spiritual activity.

Taking a deep breath, I turned the doorknob. It didn't budge.

"Try this," Jane said. She joined me on the porch and threw a rock at the window. It shattered, the sound reverberating in the night.

"Now we've all just committed a felony," Simon said. "I won't make it in prison."

This was all apparently way more than Mary bargained for.

"I shouldn't be here," she said. "I'm almost an honors student."

Jane stuck her hand through the windowpane, found the lock, and opened the front door.

"At least let's go inside," she said.

The four of us huddled closely together and slowly began walking through the house.

The place was empty save for a couple of lawn chairs, old food containers, beer bottles, and various scattered debris. There were holes in the walls, a stain that eerily matched the outline of a human body, and of course, a necessary feature of all haunted houses, a bathtub placed randomly in the corner of one of the rooms.

Every sound became magnified tenfold. The wind whistled through the cracks in the windows. A tree limb banged loudly against the side of the house, forcing us closer together.

"I think I just peed a little," Simon said, forgetting he was on a date.

"Me too," Mary said. "Okay, a lot."

Our four cellphone flashlights moved around the room, barely piercing the darkness. We took the collective power of the light and shined it on a wall at the back of the house.

"Hieroglyphics," Simon said, pointing to the wall full of spray-painted insignia.

Together, we went over to get a closer look.

"What were they trying to tell us," I said, looking at the penises and various other vulgarities.

"It's in an ancient dialect," Simon said.

"Who is this Carl, and what type of good time does he have in mind?"

By the time I turned around, Jane had disappeared.

"Jane?" I said tentatively.

I heard the stairs creak.

"Grandma?" Mary said to no one in particular.

My heart started racing, and I walked over to the stairs, intent on retrieving Jane, even if it meant fighting through a barrage of paranormal activity.

"Jane," I whispered at the foot of the steps.

"Come on," she said. I saw the light of her cellphone at the top of the stairs.

I reluctantly followed, trailing the light of her phone.

Once I reached the top, Jane and I tiptoed through the hallway, holding hands, every noise making us tighten our grip. We stopped at a closed door all the way at the end, which I assumed was McCallen's bedroom, the inner chamber, the source and cure of Burgerville's insanity.

I felt Jane's breath on my neck.

"Should we?" she said, tilting her head toward the closed door.

"I don't think that's a good idea," I said.

Something banged against the door, like it was trying to get out.

"I guess he's waiting for us," Jane said. She reached for the doorknob. The door slowly creaked open, revealing a pitch-black interior.

Jane angled her flashlight into the room and walked in. I peered through the doorway. In the middle of the room, there was an old pair of boots, as if someone had just disintegrated mid-step.

I followed Jane, not sure what to expect. The wind picked up, slamming against the wooden boards covering the windows. "Were you expecting an appointment with McCallen?"

Jane shrugged. "I didn't know *what* to expect. That's part of the fun."

"You know, we do have real therapists in Burgerville," I said. I tried to make it sound like a joke, but the minute I said it, I knew I'd made a mistake. My voice betrayed my true intentions; the shaky delivery, fake laugh. So much for subtlety.

"What's that supposed to mean?"

"Nothing. Just making a joke."

Jane paced around, examining the debris on the floor, kicking the rubble with her black boots. "Have I ever shown you a picture of Ellie?" she asked.

I shook my head. Jane scrolled through a few photos on her phone and then handed it to me, the screen frozen on a picture of two girls.

For so long I'd wondered about what Jane was like before moving to Burgerville, and now, there she was. The same dark hair. A little bit more makeup. Slightly younger. But there was something about her that looked lighter.

Next to her, their faces smooshed together, there was a girl with dark skin and red-streaked hair, just like Jane's. She had on a Bigfoot T-shirt that said: *Don't feed the wildlife.*

I handed her back the phone.

"Why don't you two hang out anymore?"

"I moved to Burgerville," she said.

"Yeah, but it doesn't seem like you two talk. What happened?"

"We just don't talk, okay?"

I let it go. I was worried if I kept pushing, Jane would stop telling me anything at all.

The light from her phone flickered across the walls, the ceiling, the debris on the floor. "This is where he hanged himself, isn't it?"

"That's what they say."

"We look back and know that using leeches and draining people's blood was a bad idea. That you can't just pray for a cure. But with depression and stuff, people still act like something's wrong with *you*. That you're choosing it or something. But they're not. *I'm* not, okay?"

"I know," I said, though if I'm telling the truth I didn't really know. I didn't know anything. "I never said you were."

"Because if I could choose, trust me, I wouldn't choose to be stuck with this."

This. I still wasn't even sure what *this* was for Jane. I didn't know what to say. I was beginning to realize that Jane needed more help than my random images.

"Maybe you should tell McCallen," I said.

"Tell him what?"

"What you *would* choose."

"I wouldn't wake up feeling sad," she said quietly. "I'd stop feeling like such a bad luck charm. I'd—"

Just then, we heard a car pull into the driveway. A look of panic spread across Jane's face, and I almost joined Simon and Mary's club of people who pee their pants. Okay, fine, it wasn't almost.

With barely any time to think about what was happening, we sprinted down the stairs, where Simon and Mary waited at the front door. The red and blue lights of a police car flashed outside, bathing the house in intermittent bursts of color.

"I'm going to surrender," Simon said.

"This isn't a shootout," I said.

"My parents are never going to let me go on another date with you," Mary said, her voice wavering.

"You wanted to go on another date?" Simon said.

"Stay calm," Jane said. "Follow my lead."

Two flashlights approached, zeroing in on the broken window.

"We're in here, Officer," Simon yelled.

Jane glared at Simon. "I said *follow my lead*." She walked to the front door and opened it, no different than if she were hosting a dinner party. Two police officers stood there, a fat one and a skinny one, their flashlights shining directly into Jane's face.

Jane shielded her eyes.

"There was something up there," Jane said. "It was terrible." She started to cry, a theatrical sob that sounded similar to a child who thinks they've seen the bogeyman. Simon and I looked on, baffled. Mary was on the verge of tears herself.

The officers exchanged glances. "What'd you see?" the fat one said.

"The ghost of McCallen," Jane said.

"Is he the one who broke the window?" the skinny officer asked.

"Are any of you carrying drugs or a weapon?" the fat one said. We all shook our heads as if being controlled by a puppeteer.

"I have to take pills for gas," Simon said. "Just in case," he added, turning to Mary.

"Everything out of your pockets," the skinny officer said.

We all did as we were told, dumping the contents of our pockets onto the floor: keys, Simon's pills, our wallets, the fortune cookie I'd taken from the restaurant.

Simon seemed reluctant to take an item out of his pocket.

"Let's go," the skinny officer shouted at Simon.

"I don't think that's a good idea," Simon said.

"Now!" the skinny officer barked.

Simon pulled out a bright yellow wrapper and let it fall to the floor.

We all gasped as the light from the flashlights hit the square package. The police officers laughed. Mary blushed.

"It was my dad's. I didn't think anything was going to happen," he said, assuring Mary.

The condom had lightened the mood enough to allow Jane to distract the officers once again.

"Can we get out of here?" she asked. "This place gives me the creeps."

The skinny officer called into his radio. "Four teenagers, broken window, apparent sighting of the ghost of A. J. McCallen." He raised his eyebrows.

"This house isn't a safe place," the fat one said. "And I don't mean because of ghosts. There could be people using drugs, squatters, anything. You have to be more careful. Especially you, Latex."

Yes, we absolutely called Simon Latex for the next few weeks.

Relieved that we weren't in handcuffs, we followed the police officers outside.

The police took all of us home that night. My mom was waiting for me at the front door in her bathrobe, her hair tangled and matted like an old wig someone had found in the basement and put on crooked. After the inevitable lecture on responsibility and good decisions and how guilty I would have felt if Simon was eaten by a bear, I received my punishment: snow-shoveling duty for the rest of the year—for the whole street, helping out Gus the Partially Blind Snowman. I'm not being offensive; it was actually written on his truck.

For the rest of the night, I tossed and turned, but it wasn't the ghost of McCallen haunting me. It was Jane, her face lit up like a jack-o'-lantern, standing inside the dark unknown of McCallen's bedroom. Hiding something. Needing something I didn't know how to give her.

224 DAYS AFTER

HOME SICK

Now that Christmas vacation is over, I have to find creative ways to stay home from school. I'll pretend I have a sore throat, a fever, a stuffy noise, and when I'm feeling really creative, I'll throw in a disease from the Middle Ages, something like the King's Evil or the Bubonic Plague.

I've been out of school most of the week with Water Elf Disease, an affliction from the Middle Ages said to be caused by a witch stabbing you—at least that's what I told my mom. She's finding my jokes about random diseases less and less funny.

I hear a knock at the door.

Expecting my mom, I yell out, "I'm still under quarantine."

"Ray?"

But it's not my mom's voice. It's a voice I heard through a very different door a little over a year ago. Tommy Beddington.

"Come in," I say, not sure what to expect. This had to be the work of a school guidance counselor or some sort of community service program for popular kids.

The door creaks open. Beddington has on his letterman jacket and is wearing the same stone-faced expression as his grandfather Earl. He scans my room, taking in the full view of my little world.

"How're you feeling, man? Your mom said you had some incurable disease from the Middle Ages?"

"Don't worry, I've already ingested a lot of different plants and prayed for a cure, so it's probably not contagious."

Tommy nods, like he can't quite figure out whether I'm kidding or not. "Can I sit?"

"Go ahead."

He takes a seat on the edge of my bed. "I've been wanting to talk to you for a while now, but I didn't know what to say."

He rocks back and forth like a person on a mattress commercial trying to spill a glass of wine.

"Jane was the first person I came out to," he says after an awkward pause. "Well, except for Steven, obviously."

"You're still together?"

"I love him," he says. "I know it shouldn't matter, but I don't know, I'm afraid of what everyone would say. Sometimes I even worry about what my grandfather would think."

"He thought he saw a green mutant cow. I don't think you have to worry about him judging you."

"Well, it is possible he saw one."

"I guess," I say. It's kind of heartwarming to hear the Beddingtons still defending their patriarch.

"But that's not why I'm here," he says. "I came here to talk about Jane."

Was my face on the front page of the newspaper or something? A big picture with the caption: *Lonely Teen Seeks At-Home Friend Visits.*

I turn around to face my computer, fall into the comfortable glow of a pixelated world.

"I've been going through all our conversations thinking about how I could have done something different."

"Me too," I say.

"I feel guilty," he says.

"You shouldn't." But it doesn't sound convincing.

The mattress squeaks as he gets off the bed.

When I turn around, I realize he's looking at my spelling bee trophy, holding it in his hand, straining to read the inscription. His jacket is open in the middle, revealing a V-neck T-shirt and a gold chain hanging around his neck. His hair's slicked back, each strand perfectly in place, the kind of look only attainable through copious amounts of gel.

"This thing's got some weight to it," he says before placing it back down.

"Thanks," I say. "My crowning achievement. That and being born."

"A trophy is a trophy," he says.

"I spelled *hippopotamus*."

"That's a tough word."

I nod. An awkward pause.

"I miss her," he says.

"Me too," I say.

"We can't forget about her," Tommy says.

Without warning, he walks toward me and wraps his arms around me. A big bear hug. I sit frozen in my computer chair, counting the seconds until it stops.

Ten, nine, eight, seven . . .

But around five, I let myself melt into the hug. And it feels . . .

nice. Like he understands what I'm going through. And we didn't have to talk about history or sports or Puddinggate.

I pat him on the back. He pulls away. His face is red, puffy, snot dribbling out of his nose. I wasn't the only one hurting. Jane had left her imprint on Burgerville.

"I'm glad I came," Tommy says. "If you're feeling better, you should stop by the game."

"Game?"

"Big basketball game in Centerville. I actually gotta go catch the bus." He looks in the mirror, wipes his eyes with his jacket sleeve.

"Good luck," I say. "I'd go, but . . ." I look around my room, trying to think of an excuse, but nothing comes.

Tommy must realize I'm trying to find a way out, because he lets me off the hook. "Maybe next time."

Once he's gone, I open the drawer where I've stashed all of my Jane memorabilia: the folk CD, her folded-up drawings, random objects from our tour of Burgerville. That's when I see the crushed fortune cookie from our night at O'Reilly's, still unopened. It's like a secret message from Jane.

I carefully open it and fish out the little strip of paper.

If you think you're going to sum up your whole life on this little bit of paper, you're crazy.

"Jane," I say out loud. I start to laugh. I say her name again, laughing even harder, like it's the funniest joke I've ever heard. Jane mocking me through a fortune cookie.

My mom hesitantly walks into the room. "Ray? Is everything okay?"

But all I can do is laugh.

"Ray?"

She takes a seat on the bed and puts her arm around me.

Maybe I am crazy, because for the first time in a long time, I feel like there really is still more to learn about Jane. More to cobble together from my fragmented sources. If I want to know the real Jane, maybe I just have to do more research.

229 DAYS AFTER

ROSETTA STONE

Rich thinks I'm lonely.

"No shit I'm lonely," I tell him after I've recounted my visit with Tommy Beddington, what he'd described as "progress."

"Why are you punishing yourself? You're keeping yourself from moving forward."

The inevitable stare-down follows. Rich waiting for me to acknowledge he's right, me waiting for the awkwardness to become too much to handle.

Rich shifts in his chair, a clear sign he's switching tactics. "How are things going with your mom?" he asks.

"Fine."

"And Tim?"

"Okay, I guess." I don't want to say it out loud, but he's kind of growing on me.

"It's normal to have mixed feelings about Tim. A lot of the kids I see—"

"You see a lot of people my age?" I interrupt.

Rich nods. "I'm pretty much the only game in town."

A thought occurs to me then, and I know Rich can tell what I'm thinking, because he starts flipping through his notepad, checking his watch, anything to avoid eye contact.

"Then you would have known Jane," I say.

An uncomfortable silence settles over the room. The possibility that the entire time I'd been talking to Rich he'd also known Jane feels like a great discovery, no different from uncovering King Tut's Tomb or the Rosetta Stone. Maybe I've finally found the key to help me unlock all of Jane's secrets.

"You know I can't talk about that, Ray."

His voice sounds small, as if coming from underwater. Anger wells up inside of me. The excitement of discovery has worn off, and I'm left feeling betrayed; Rich has had the answers I needed all along.

"Did she talk about me?" I ask.

Rich's face stays buried in his papers, his mouth closed. His head slightly moves up and down.

"That's a yes?"

Rich steadies his head. "I can't, Ray. I'm sorry."

"Anything," I say. "She must have talked about me."

I spring out of my chair and rush toward him, stopping only a few feet away.

"Come on," I say. "It's not a big secret. Do sign language, burp, I don't care . . . Just give me *something*."

Rich gets out of his chair and puts his hand on my shoulder.

"There's nothing new to find out," he says.

The room starts spinning. I'm either on the verge of collapsing or ripping his office apart.

"But maybe there's something I didn't see before. I need to understand why she did it."

"Take a seat, Ray," Rich says, attempting to guide me to a chair. I shrug him off. "Get off of me!"

"I understand you're angry," Rich says. "Let's get in touch with that anger. Let's give it a voice."

But I don't want to be angry. I want answers. I want things to make sense. I want Jane. I walk past him, into the waiting room, and down the stairs.

123–112 DAYS BEFORE

VALENTINE'S DAY

By February of last year, it was becoming hard to even go a day without seeing Jane. With my mom still sore about the whole episode with the police, I sometimes had to make up stories to get out of the house. I'd pretend to go to the library to work on school projects, act as if we were missing some essential food product that warranted a trip to the grocery store ("We have no pudding in the fridge"), or insist Simon urgently needed my help ("He thinks he's been bitten by a vampire and I'm the only one who can calm him down").

Sometimes I'd pick up Jane and we'd just drive around. Jane would look out the window, staring at her reflection, as we made loops around Burgerville, traversing centuries and miles in the span of only a few hours.

"Should I bring you home?" I'd ask her.

She'd squeeze my leg or shrug or I'd see an almost imperceptible shake of the head.

One night, I asked her what she was thinking about.

"You really want to know?"

"I really want to know."

"In no particular order: I'm thinking about whatever happened to blue ketchup. How unfair it is that dolphins don't have vocal cords. Something I don't want to talk about. Another thing I don't want to talk about. How much it would suck if I didn't get to see you anymore. Where are the Teletubbies today? Are they like horrible drug addicts or just regular people walking around with this phenomenal secret that—"

I pulled the car over and stopped on the side of the street.

"Why wouldn't you get to see me anymore?"

Jane turned away from her reflection. We were on the outskirts of Burgerville in the Shank, near the big farms. The faint scent of manure—Burgerville's town smell—wafted through the car.

"Life is unpredictable," she said.

"Hey," I said. "A tyrannosaurus rex giving birth to Mr. Rogers."

"Thanks," Jane said. "I needed that."

She leaned across the cup holders, held my face with her hands, and kissed me, accidentally hitting pretty much every button in my mom's car. But I barely noticed. We continued to make out while the windshield wipers scraped back and forth, the hazard lights blinked, and the radio blared Burgerville's local political station.

We took a break from kissing. "Seriously, though, you know I'm not going anywhere, right?"

"I know *you're* not."

"What's that supposed to mean?" My voice cracked. Was she thinking about breaking up with me? Was her family moving again? Or . . . I didn't even let my mind go there.

"Relax," Jane said. "I'm just saying that alien abductions happen all the time."

"Don't say things like that."

"It's true. Even though the government wants to pretend—"

"I'm not talking about the aliens."

"I know."

With Valentine's Day just around the corner, Jane warned me not to do anything to celebrate the holiday. "Whatever you have planned," she said, "cancel it."

"No horse-drawn carriage?"

"Don't even joke about that," she said.

"Can we at least go to dinner?"

"Only if we split the check," she said.

"Flowers?"

"Absolutely not."

"Chocolate?"

"We can share a non-chocolate dessert."

"Deal."

When Valentine's Day finally arrived, Simon came over to my house to get ready. Even though we had separate plans, Simon thought it would be a good idea to meet up beforehand to talk "strategy," which really meant he was nervous and needed something to take his mind off all the ways his date with Mary could go wrong.

But as Jane was proud to point out, it appeared we had made the perfect match. After our trip to the McCallen Mansion, Simon and Mary had gone on a couple more dates, first to the Renaissance Faire, where they jousted with each other, and then to a book signing by Simon's favorite vampire author, a woman who always wears fangs and black-tinted contact lenses. After the signing, Simon and Mary kissed for the first time, fake vampire fangs and all. I'd never seen Simon so excited.

"Can you believe this?" Simon said, standing in front of my mirror, nodding approvingly at his outfit.

"Believe what?"

"That we both have dates," he said. "It's a miracle."

"It's not a miracle," I said. "This is the way life's supposed to be."

I walked over to the mirror so Simon and I were standing shoulder to shoulder and began putting the final touches on my hair. I smoothed out my collar and sprayed myself with a bottle of something Simon had taken from his dad's bathroom.

"The more of that stuff, the better," Simon said, grabbing the bottle and spraying a suffocating cloud as he turned around in a circle. "Women can't resist."

My mom came to the door, choking a little on the cloud of cologne.

"Look at you two," she said. "So handsome."

Simon blushed. "Thanks, Mrs. Green."

I glimpsed her in the mirror and realized she was dressed up as well: black dress, hair done up, the earrings she only wore when someone died or got married.

"And may I say you look beautiful yourself," Simon said.

The little creep.

She smiled. "Tim will be here any minute."

I thought I'd be angry. But I didn't think about my dad in Florida or the divorce or the fact that this night felt somehow symbolic, a chapter closed on our old life. Instead, I just felt happy for her.

My mom placed her car keys on the dresser. "Be careful," she said, an edge to her voice, a tone I'd grown used to ever since the police brought me home from the McCallen Mansion. "Back by twelve."

I heard Tim open the front door. "Ready?" he called up.

"We're in Ray's room," she yelled.

Tim climbed the stairs.

"Hey, Bud," he said, appearing outside the doorway.

"Hey, Tim," I said.

"I see you have your sidekick with you," he said.

"This is Simon," I said.

"The legendary Simon," Tim said, coughing as he entered the room.

Simon looked starstruck. Tim, dressed in khakis and a nice button-down shirt, his hair gelled, did cut an impressive image. Simon gulped.

"We'll be back early," my mom said. She walked over to me and straightened out my collar. "Have fun." Her voice trailed off; she cleared her throat and sniffled.

"Are you crying?" I asked, watching her in the mirror.

Tim pulled out a handkerchief and handed it to her. She shielded her face with her hand.

"It's just . . ." She blew her nose. The mascara started running down her cheeks.

"All right," I said, rolling my eyes. "Not in front of the kids." I motioned to Simon.

She collected herself, dabbing at her eyes with Tim's handkerchief.

Something about how she leaned into Tim made me feel guilty.

Just as she was about to turn around and leave the room, I heard myself begin to speak.

"Have fun," I said. "And"—taking a deep breath—"I love you."

My mom tilted her head, as if she wasn't sure she heard me correctly. "I love you too," she said. "See you boys later." Tim put his arm around her, waved, then escorted her out of the room.

"Are you dying?" Simon asked.

"She gets weird like that sometimes. First day of high school, first B on my report card, you know, big life milestones."

"Luckily she has Tim to comfort her."

"I don't want to talk about it."

Simon sprayed a little bit more cologne. "He's the size of a football player," he said, gazing off into space. "What size shoe do you think he has?"

"Simon!"

"Sorry."

"How do I look?" I asked, turning around to face him.

"Like a million bucks," he said, "adjusted for inflation. How about me?"

Simon had gotten rid of the T-shirt tux and was actually wearing a blazer.

"Looking smooth, Latex, real smooth."

We traded a couple more compliments, then went our separate ways, two guys from the wrong side of the bone who'd finally found the right dimension.

112 DAYS BEFORE, CONT'D

AFFIRMATIONS

On the way to Jane's house that Valentine's Day, the full moon followed me like a spotlight. In Burgerville, a full moon is said to "exert a gravitational force on history"—at least according to Roger Lutz, who first connected the moon to Burgerville's history in his classic 1971 essay, "Men on the Moon: The Lunar History of Burgerville."

Most people dismiss his theory as pseudo-history, a fantasy/science-fiction hybrid that not even the Burgerville Historical Association can get behind. I'd normally agree with them, but when I look back on my brief time with Jane, there's one fact I can't ignore: Whenever there was a full moon, something changed about our relationship.

As I approached Jane's driveway, I felt the weight of the moment; but for once it was the weight of the future.

I parked and walked to the porch. Before I had the chance to knock, Mrs. Doe opened the door. Mr. Doe sat behind her, anxiously peering at the stairs. They spoke in hushed tones, as if they were trying not to wake Jane.

"Jane's upstairs getting ready," Mrs. Doe said.

"Can we talk to you for a minute?" Mr. Doe asked.

I started sweating. Nothing good ever came out of a private chat with your girlfriend's parents. The Does had never said anything to me about the episode with the police, but Jane's whereabouts were now monitored more closely, her curfew set well before midnight. I worried that they had begun to view me as a bad influence in their daughter's life. Part of me felt complimented that anyone could think of me—a person who up until a few months ago thought a rum and Coke was a "Roman Coke"—as a threat to their child. But I was afraid the Does would grow restless and move Jane once again.

The mood was somber. Mr. Doe's motor even gave off a sad droning as he led the way to the nearby study.

"I'm sorry about the whole thing with the police," I said. "It was all my fault."

Mr. Doe looked at me like he didn't know what I was talking about. "Oh, that. You guys made a mistake. We trust you, Ray."

"Compared to . . ." Mrs. Doe's voice trailed off. She paused and collected herself. "As you know, Jane hasn't had an easy couple of years," Mrs. Doe said. "Ever since . . ." Her voice faded once again; she looked uncertainly to Mr. Doe.

"She's been happy here," Mr. Doe said.

Happy was not exactly the way I'd describe Jane. It made me think, Happy compared to what?

"But she's still got a long way to go," Mrs. Doe said.

"If you notice anything out of the ordinary," Mr. Doe jumped in, "just give us a call."

"I will." I looked around the study, trying to avoid eye contact with Mr. Doe. It was hard enough talking to Jane about this stuff; now I felt like I had to know the right thing to say to her parents too. As I scanned the room, I noticed pictures of Mr. Doe doing all sorts of athletic activities: Throwing a shotput. Running along a track. Doing the pole vault.

"I was All-American in college," he said, following my gaze to a picture of him jumping through the air, legs kicking, long hair flowing behind him.

I wondered if that was part of the reason Jane felt so guilty. If these pictures had to be locked away in a study so she wouldn't see them.

"But Jane's mom was the real talent. For a while she even held the college record for the ten thousand meter. We actually met on the track. Do you run?"

"Only if a green cow is chasing me," I said.

Mrs. Doe laughed. "We've tried to get Jane into running, but she's never been the athletic type."

"I assume Jane told you about the car accident?" Mr. Doe said.

"A little."

"I know she blames herself, even though I've told her a million times it had nothing to do with her."

Our attention was taken to the sound of footsteps slowly descending the stairs.

"Anyway," Mr. Doe said. "Let's keep this conversation between us."

We left the room and met Jane. Her dark hair fanned out over her shoulders; the red streaks had faded, making her look more like a girl who'd grown up in Burgerville. She wore a slim-fitting black dress, in stark contrast to her usual wardrobe of obscure folk tees, and had forgone her customary assortment of bracelets, instead settling on only one, strategically placed to cover up the scar on her wrist. I didn't have the normal reaction, the type of Hollywood moment where the stalkerish love song plays over the couple locking eyes as time slows down. Instead, I felt woefully inadequate, as if Jane had made a horrible mistake.

"Don't say anything," Jane said.

I remained speechless.

"One picture," Jane said to her mom, completely unprompted. Mrs. Doe reached into the back of Mr. Doe's chair and took out a camera.

"Say 'cheese,'" Mrs. Doe said.

We said nothing.

"Hop in," Mr. Doe said, pointing to the back of his scooter.

"I think Ray's driving," Jane said, as if her dad was serious about the offer.

We said good-bye to Jane's parents, both of them tearing up like my mom had, and made our way outside.

"No flowers?" Jane asked me as we were leaving.

I stuttered. "I thought—"

"I'm kidding."

We walked to my car. Jane opened the passenger-side door, where I had placed a bouquet of a dozen roses.

She picked the bouquet off the seat, smelled the flowers, and placed them across her lap.

"Do you like them?"

"No," she said.

"The florist said you can't go wrong with roses."

"The florist was right," Jane said, her head turned toward the window.

On the drive over to the restaurant, all I could think about was what Jane's parents had said about keeping an eye out for her. She was quiet, engaged in a tense stare-down with her reflection, where losing was inevitable.

"Music?"

Jane nodded.

I turned the volume up quickly, not stopping to consider what my mom had left on the radio.

"You are perfect just the way you are," a calm voice said through the speakers. Waterfalls in the background. A harp playing what could only be described as the music you might hear at the gates of heaven, if such a thing actually existed.

"You deserve to be loved," the voice said.

My mom had been listening to these types of things ever since my dad left. She would never actually play them with me in the car, but at home I could sometimes hear her having a muffled conversation with a faceless stranger, the two of them content with simply saying the same thing back to each other.

"Whoops," I said.

Jane continued to stare at her reflection.

I reached for the dial.

"Leave it," she said.

I drove on, both of us silent, listening to an old woman describe how great she was, entreating us to do the same. I don't know why, but at some point, I decided to join in.

Old Woman: "I am beautiful because I am me."

Me: "I am beautiful because I am me."

Jane turned away from her reflection.

Old Woman: "I am kind and loving, and attract kind and loving people into my life."

"This is bizarre," Jane said.

"My mom loves these," I said, talking over the blank space where we were supposed to be repeating after the old sage.

Old Woman: "I am exactly where I need to be."

"But what if you're not?" Jane asked. The sounds of nature accompanied by a harp answered Jane.

"It makes people feel good," I said, talking over the old woman.

"But it's a lie," Jane said.

"It's only a lie if you believe it is."

"It's the equivalent of believing in magic," Jane said.

"Your life is a miracle," the voice said.

"There's your answer, Jane."

In response, Jane hit the radio dial. It so happened that my mom's other listening habits were classic rock. Hendrix's distorted guitar blared through the radio as Jane let her head fall back onto the headrest.

"*That's* the answer."

I rolled down my window, letting the cold air pour into the car. Maybe the affirmations were magic after all, because I saw Jane's face soften as her scowl turned into a smile.

112 DAYS BEFORE, CONT'D

BE HAPPY

I'd made reservations at a restaurant across the street from O'Reilly's called Pisa Pizza. As the only Italian restaurant in Burgerville, it served multiple roles, from your typical pizzeria to upscale dining on special occasions.

When we arrived, the restaurant was packed with couples moving steadily through their meals. Leaning Tower of Pisa candle holders were placed in the middle of each table, a fire hazard to be sure, but also oddly elegant in their imperfection. The usual red-checkered tablecloths were replaced by white linen and the lighting had changed from pizza parlor bright to cave-dweller dim. The staff buzzed around the tables like bees pollinating flowers, though the typical T-shirt, jeans, and surly expressions had been swapped out for black ties and fawning grins. Everything had the air of efficiency: the speed with which we sat at our table, the follow-up drink order, the quick return of the waiter asking if we'd had enough time to look over the menu. Valentine's Day is big business; love is only incidental.

While we waited for our food, Jane seemed to be in good spirits, at one point even leaning across the table to feed me a piece of bread.

"I feel like a baby bird," I said.

"Way to ruin the moment," Jane said.

I contorted my lips into something that resembled a beak and let out a high-pitched squeal.

"I don't think I'll be able to get that image out of my head," Jane said. "Might as well just call it a night."

"Lesson learned. Baby bird impersonations are not sexy."

"I didn't say that," Jane said.

Soon after, our dinner arrived. Eggplant Parmesan for me, lasagna for Jane.

We were quiet for a few minutes, listening to the chatter of couples sharing romantic moments around us: professing love, renewing vows, complaining about the soggy fried calamari, how it was mostly tentacles, and that next time they were definitely going to say something.

Jane poked at her lasagna, watching tomato sauce billow out like lava from a volcano. Something about the dim interior and Jane's expression—somewhere between thoughtful and self-conscious—just got to me.

"I think I love you," I said. It was an accident. I mean, it was true, but I didn't mean to say it out loud.

Jane looked up from her lasagna. "You think?"

I backtracked. "I don't know," I said. "Sorry."

"But do you?"

"I think I do."

"Thanks," she said.

"You're welcome," I said.

Jane smiled. "I think I love you too." She looked away, as if the moment was too intense. I reached across the table and held her hand. Instead of moving it away like she usually did in public, she kept still; there was something almost challenging about her stare, like she was asking me to arm wrestle.

"I was thinking that after dinner we could take a walk around town," I said.

"How about *your* house instead?" She then gave me a look I had never seen a girl give me before.

I nodded, gulping.

I sped through dinner, eating my eggplant as if I were part of a pack and the others were waiting to steal my food. Jane seemed amused by this, as she took her time, letting herself enjoy every bite.

I ate too quickly, so by the end, I had a stomachache and was slumped down in my chair with beads of sweat on my forehead.

"Let's get out of here," Jane said, now that I could barely move.

We got into the car and I began driving home. Jane fumbled with the radio dial until the light strumming of acoustic guitar filled the car.

"Oh my god," she said. "Oh my god."

"What is it?"

"It's my grandma. Her only single."

I listened closer. Grandma Irene's voice was belting out the chorus to "Be Happy."

If you want to love the Earth,
Love yourself.
If you want to stop a war,
Find your peace.
If you want to be happy,
Be happy.

"Okay, I'll admit it," I said, glancing over at Jane in the passenger seat. "I called the radio station and planned for them to play the song at this exact moment."

Jane laughed. "You're so full of shit. I've gotta tell my mom." She took out her cellphone and started screaming when her mom picked up. "They're playing Grandma Irene on the radio!"

Jane held the phone up to the speaker. There was a brief pause followed by an ear-piercing shriek from Mrs. Doe.

It felt like some sort of catharsis, Grandma Irene speaking to Jane from across time, telling her to have hope, to love herself, to love the world. And to stop spraying horrible chemicals on our crops.

Jane hung up and let her head fall back on the headrest as she sang along.

I sped up, the music urging us on, as if it might be possible to bend time and space in order to get to my house faster. By the time the song ended, we had finally pulled into my driveway.

Jane sprinted out of the car, still humming her grandma's song. I followed her to the porch, fumbling with my house key, for some reason unable to fit it into the lock. I was considering ramming my shoulder into the door when Jane gently touched my wrist. I realized my hand was shaking.

"Relax," she said.

She took my keychain and easily slid the key into the lock. Taking me by the hand, she pulled me inside. I took a deep breath as Jane led me through the kitchen and up the stairs.

Once we got to my room, Jane kicked off her shoes and went to lie down on my bed.

"Food coma," she said.

I stumbled across the room, pretending to be drunk on eggplant. I lay down next to her and wrapped her up in my arms. Jane pulled me even closer. "I never thought living in Burgerville would be a good thing," she said, almost like she was just realizing it now. "But these past few months have felt like a reset. It's like I feel almost . . . normal."

"You're *so* normal," I said. "And we're as normal as a couple gets. Extremely normal. Eat-at-the-diner-without-speaking normal."

"Go-on-vacation-to-Disney-World normal?"

"Talk-about-the-police-blotter-while-eating-cantaloupe normal," I said.

I moved closer. Our noses pressed up against each other's, her face a blur. We started kissing.

She pulled her dress over her head and then threw it across the room. I stood up and stripped down to my boxers, wiggling my legs to escape my pants as Jane pretended to check her imaginary watch.

"It's harder than it looks," I said. Jane rolled her eyes and pulled me into bed, the mattress springs squealing as we rebounded and collapsed beside each other. Jane slid underneath the comforter and before I knew it I saw her bra and underwear join her dress in a crumpled pile on the floor.

I reached for my bedside table and grabbed one of the bright yellow wrappers Simon had stolen from his dad.

I fumbled around, trying to find the right end. Jane coached me through it, the process feeling painfully like a video you'd watch in health class.

Finally, I joined Jane under the covers. I worried our bodies might suddenly burst into flames, or I'd have an asthma attack, or I'd wake up in a cold sweat sucking my thumb. It all seemed too good to be true.

"Well, I guess I should be getting home," Jane said.

"It *is* getting late," I said, out of breath, tracing lines down Jane's arm.

"I wouldn't want to be out past curfew." She rubbed her hand over my chest.

"You better go," I said.

She pressed closer to me and our lips touched, just briefly, and then her arms were around my shoulders. Hands grasping at my back. Finally her legs wrapped around me, and it was like we were one person—two people with two histories now somehow condensed into one.

No past, no future, only Jane and me, an infinity that was compressed into a couple of minutes.

Afterward, I wondered if I had done it right. All of those voices in my head once again competing for time: *It wasn't long enough. You were breathing like a lawn mower. What the hell was that thrusting move you tried to do in the final stretch?*

But when I voiced some of my concerns, Jane simply shook her head and rested her finger on my lips. "It was perfect." We were both quiet for a moment. "And you're perfect," she added in the cheerful voice of my mom's affirmation CD. "Just for being you."

"Can I get a recording of you saying that?"

"Sure, but it's gonna cost you." Jane sat up. "Should we get going?"

I looked at the clock, suddenly aware of time rushing forward. I didn't want the night to end. "We have a little bit longer," I said, pulling Jane back into bed. "My mom won't be back for at least another hour."

We lay under the covers for a long time, every exchange punctuated by a kiss: "I'm feeling this strong desire to make pledges to you. About love and eternity and playing backgammon together."

Kiss!

"You sound a little bit like a stalker. But for some reason, I'm okay with that."

Kiss!

At one point, I accidentally ran my finger over her wrist. The bracelet had slid down her arm, leaving her scar exposed. Her body jerked. She immediately pulled her bracelet back up.

"You don't have to be embarrassed," I said.

She let her hand relax. I held her wrist, running my finger over the raised skin. The scar wasn't like any scar I'd ever seen before. It looked like a small mountain range, ridges and peaks, a deep valley in between. The skin was still pink in some places.

"Pretty ugly, huh?"

"No," I said. I brought her wrist to my lips and kissed her scar. "There's nothing ugly about you."

I guess we lost track of time, because a little while later, we heard a car pull into the driveway. I glanced at the clock and saw that it was already past eleven. Jane and I sprung out of bed and threw our clothes on. My mom was cool, but she wasn't girlfriend-alone-in-the-room cool.

"Shit," I said.

"Calm down," Jane said. But by the tone of her voice I could tell she was just as freaked out as I was.

"I'll hide under the bed," Jane said.

"I'm a horrible liar," I said. "I'd probably give you up."

"We could . . ." Jane nodded to the window. The branches tapped against the glass from a light breeze.

"I've never snuck out," I said.

"Your call," she said. "Wait for your mom or . . ." She paused. "Escape."

The front door opened.

"Ray?" my mom yelled up the stairs.

"Let's go," I said. I grabbed my phone, straightened out my comforter, and buried the condom wrapper in the trash.

Jane crawled out the window, took hold of a branch, and lowered herself to the ground. I hesitated, surveying my room one last time. Knowing there was no turning back, I leaped to the tree, the branches like little fingers scraping against the side of the house.

Jane started running, past my yard and out into the street.

I trailed behind her, the cold night air rushing through my hair.

"Where are you going?" I called.

"It doesn't matter," Jane yelled back.

I followed, the two of us running as fast as we could. Something came over me, and I felt the need to scream in celebration, as if we'd just escaped certain death. I attempted a Beddington green cow howl, something every kid in Burgerville learns in elementary school. Jane laughed and joined in, until we were both mooing at the top of our lungs. We kept going until we arrived at Beddington's statue, the site of our first date.

"We made it," Jane said.

Beddington's gaze remained focused on Green Cow Acres. Clouds hovered at the edge of the horizon.

"My mom's going to kill me," I said.

"At least now you won't die a virgin," she said.

"Good point."

We sat down in front of Beddington, our backs resting against the base of the statue, as my phone began to vibrate in my pocket, the energy of an angry mother transformed into a digital scream. Just like our first date all those months ago, I felt Jane lean into me, only now the entire weight of her body pressed against me.

"Tonight was so cliché," Jane said.

"What are you talking about? No chocolates. No horse-drawn carriage. Only a couple sappy speeches—"

"I loved it," Jane said.

I called Simon and he picked us up a little while later. Instead of sneaking out, he told his parents he needed to go to the store to grab some milk—always believable in Simon's case. When he arrived, we silently thanked Beddington for the hospitality and piled into the back of the Red Rocket.

"Where's Mary?" I asked.

"She had to go home." A smile spread across his lips.

"How was dinner?"

"We never made it to the restaurant."

I tapped him on the shoulder, smiling.

"It's a miracle," Jane said.

"Hey," Simon said, "any girl would be lucky to take my virginity."

"Not that you lost your virginity," Jane shot back. "That somehow we all found each other." Simon drove on, the moon hidden behind the clouds moving in from Murphy. A silence settled over the car and I had the strangest feeling that we were taking off, gravity loosening its grip as we hurtled through space.

243 DAYS AFTER

THE CAR METHOD

Rich's favorite new acronym is CAR, which stands for Change, Accept, Reframe. He likes it because, in his words, the CAR method is "a vehicle that gets you where you need to be."

At which point I gag, then promptly apologize and blame it on a bad case of acid reflux.

"Say what you want," Rich says. "I've already seen the CAR method do a lot of good for my other clients. You can stand on the side of the road all you want."

"What's that supposed to mean?"

"You tell me," he says.

We become locked in an epic stare-down.

"You're right," I finally say, looking away. I'm tired of pretending.

"What?" Rich says, surprised.

"I have to take some little steps, right?"

He passes me a worksheet with *Copyright Richard Dawson* written all over it. "That's right," he says hesitantly, as if it's all an elaborate setup for a punch line and green slime is about to pour on his head. "You've gotta take some little steps . . . and maybe I can give you a ride along the way."

Problem #1: Simon and I aren't nearly as close as we used to be. We didn't go to the homeless shelter in Murphy, we didn't hang out over Christmas, and we've only watched one horror movie since the beginning of the school year: *Founding Monsters,* a historical saga that asks the burning question "What if the Founding Fathers were actually bloodthirsty vampires?" It's not like we had a big fight or anything, it's just that things are different without Jane.

    _X_ Change

    ____ Accept

    ____ Reframe

Next steps: I guess I can reach out to Simon and invite him over to watch another horror movie. There's one I'd like to see about a hybrid vampire-bear that terrorizes a small village in the Midwest, which of course raises the question of how the monster came to be. Eek. It's called *Count Grizzly.*

Problem #2: Rich's new goatee. It's one of those things that sound great on paper but doesn't work in reality.

    ____ Change

    ____ Accept

    _X_ Reframe

Next steps: I have to understand that Rich is a grown man and if he wants to have a goatee and alienate his wife and kids and potentially his clients and maybe somehow set the world of facial hair back at least fifty years, it's up to him.

Problem #3: Everything with my dad. When he moved to Florida, part of me thought it would only be temporary. He'd realize he made a mistake and come rushing back home. But a week passed, then a month, then a year, and I started to doubt the effectiveness of my Cold War–era diplomacy strategy.

  _X_ Change
  ____ Accept
  ____ Reframe

Next steps: I can reach out to him and say something cheesy like, "Let's put the past behind us." We could go to a baseball game, eat Cracker Jack, talk about how much we've both grown (for some reason I picture him with a big belly).

Problem #4: My last night with Jane.

  ____ Change
  _X_ Accept
  ____ Reframe

Next steps: Jane was right. You can't change history.

111–84 DAYS BEFORE

THE TRUTH ABOUT GRANDMA IRENE

Once Simon and Mary started dating, and both Simon and I found ourselves with girlfriends—which, according to Simon, could only mean the end of the world was near—the dynamic of our group began to change.

"We did it again," Simon told me a few days after he'd picked Jane and me up at Beddington's statue. I couldn't tell if he was letting me know he'd had sex or was confessing a crime.

"That's nice," I said.

"On the kitchen table."

We happened to be eating lunch at his kitchen table. I pushed my plate way. "Gross," I said.

"I never thought I could be so happy. How are things going with Jane, if you know what I mean?"

I wasn't entirely comfortable sharing my sex life with Simon, so I simply nodded and made up a story.

"We did it in your minivan," I said.

"Where was I?"

"I'm kidding, Simon." While I may have also thrown in a ridiculous story involving chocolate syrup and marinara sauce just to mess with Simon, the truth is, Jane and I were sneaking off whenever we had the chance. Sometimes in the car (sorry, Mom), in the basement of the library, even a few times in the Lost Woods, which I wouldn't suggest, considering I got a rash from poison ivy in an area that really makes you understand the value of underwear.

After a brief discussion about the pitfalls of mixing food and sex (a list that included third-degree burns, diabetes, and the potential dangers of Pavlov's response being translated to other situations), Simon seemed to be lost in thought. He paused and patted the kitchen table like an old friend. "Can I ask you a question about sex?"

"No," I said.

Simon asked anyway.

(The following has been edited to be PG-13 friendly. Or, if you have a pencil, it's been edited to become a game of Mad Libs.)

"When you _____ with the _____, how do you know the _____ is not _____?"

"You're a _____," I said. "You _____ and make sure to _____."

"But doesn't that hurt the _____?"

"Simon, do you even know what a _____ is?"

"Isn't a _____ a _____ located on the woman's _____?"

"I hope you're kidding."

Simon shook his head.

"I'm surprised you still have a _____."

"She seems to enjoy it," Simon rebutted.

Such were our conversations about sex.

The four of us tried to make the new dynamic work. I know, I'm probably sounding like my mom and dad, but it's true. We still hung out together whenever we could. We all went to see Mary in her debut role as a tree in the school play, or, as Simon called it, her "starring role as a tree." Simon beamed proudly, while Jane kept asking, "Which tree is Mary?"

When Simon's dad was elected to the town council, running on his Vietnam War record—not for fighting in the war, but for organizing a protest in his fourth-grade class—we all went to the victory party as a group. Mr. Blackburn made a speech about his road to vindication, from being called a traitor for his heartfelt letters to Ho Chi Minh to now being celebrated as the youngest anti-war protestor of all time.

At the party, we stood in the corner, watching the who's who of Burgerville congratulate one another on their vaunted status, the powerbrokers in a town with more cows than people.

"We're with royalty now," I said.

"The prince of Burgerville," Jane said.

"And his princess," Simon added, pulling Mary close.

Jane gagged.

We even went to the grand opening of the new O'Reilly's in Murphy, where, true to the town slogan, they ran out of silverware, so we had to eat with our hands, two cases of salmonella were reported, and the mechanical dragon that spits fire accidentally triggered the sprinkler system. Things were good.

Still, Jane sometimes seemed to be somewhere else. *Someone* else. She'd get really quiet and ask me to bring her home. I'd try to cheer her up, but in those moments, nothing seemed to work.

"An elephant with a human nose," I'd say. Or "The Flying Possum of Williamsburg wearing a leopard print leotard." Sometimes she'd smile, but other times, it was like she couldn't.

It was on one of our drives through Burgerville that I learned the truth about Grandma Irene. I was trying to cheer Jane up with her grandmother's music, but she wasn't having it.

"Maybe it really is just as simple as Grandma Irene makes it out to be," I said. "If you want to be happy, be happy."

"That's not how it works," Jane said, an edge to her voice.

"I know, but maybe part of feeling better is pretending for a little while. Maybe that's what Grandma Irene meant."

"She was just as unhappy as anyone," Jane said.

"Why? What happened?"

"My mom never tells the whole story about the Folk Williamsburg Festival," Jane said.

"There's more to it?"

"She always leaves out the ending. The town officials were worried about all the young people voting them out of power, so they passed a bunch of laws to silence them—no more big gatherings, no more tie-dye, and Grandma Irene was accused of inciting a riot. That's when she decided to move back to New York."

I thought of the portrait hanging in the Does' stairwell. The look of confusion. The happy, upbeat folk masking the truth of her sadness.

Grandma Irene continued singing, her voice bright and cheerful, as the Burgerville landscape rolled by.

"But the older I get, the more I realize that all of her happy music was just a way to trick herself," Jane said. "My grandmother was never really happy. Not back then, not ever. I remember my mom and me bringing her to doctors' appointments. The long talks with my parents explaining why Grandma Irene didn't feel like listening to music with me. And that it didn't mean she loved me any less. I didn't get it then, but I get it now. Just like it was a part of my grandma, it's a part of me."

"So I guess my random images aren't much help," I said.

"I think it's about things helping a little bit," she said. "There are no miracles in real life. It's all the little steps that make a difference. At least that's what my therapist says."

"You're seeing a therapist?" I said.

Jane nodded.

"That's good, Jane. That's really good." The happiness must have creeped into my voice, toddler taking their first steps kind of happiness, because Jane quickly said, "Jeez, I feel like I just told you I'm going to the Olympics for bobsled."

"I'm just happy, that's all. And you'd make a terrible bobsledder."

"Hey," she said.

She paused, bit her lip. "I'm taking some medicine too." She said it quietly, like she wasn't quite sure she should be telling people.

I realized how hard it must have been for her. To go around feeling like you had to be embarrassed and ashamed. That your love of folk music, your drawing, chasing conspiracy theories and weird histories—you could add all of them up, but they'd still feel less than your sadness.

"I'm proud of you," I told her as some sort of flute whistled through the speakers. "Your grandma would be proud of you too."

"Gee, thanks," she said.

"Seriously," I said.

"I know."

Out of the corner of my eye I saw her smile—a real smile, no sinister edges creeping in—before she leaned over and kissed me. We kept driving for a while after that, neither of us speaking, all the spots on our tour of Burgerville scattered around us, another reminder of just how close history could be.

251 DAYS AFTER

THE REUNION

After almost three years, my dad finally came back to visit Burgerville.

I guess my mom called him again, probably told him I could use his fatherly wisdom. Which means she must be really worried about me. Lately I've been feeling like a terminally ill patient, but without the Make-A-Wish Foundation. No national headlines, no supporters pouring in donations, no celebrities wishing me well, no towns pretending I'm a superhero for a day. I guess that's how it is for most of us. Our pain goes unnoticed, we suffer alone, and the best we can hope for is a lightened homework load.

My mom drives me to O'Reilly's to meet him. I thought about refusing to go, but like Rich is always saying, I guess I have to try, even it's only one step at a time. We stop a few buildings away from the front entrance. "Aren't you going to come in?" I ask.

"Not today," she says.

"I don't get it."

"Get what?"

"How you can think you love someone and then not stand to be in the same room as them."

"It's complicated," she says.

"That's what everyone says. But I think a lot of the time we *make* it complicated."

"I'll pick you up in a couple of hours," she says.

I stay in the car, looking at her.

"What, Ray?" she snaps.

"You have the child lock on."

Her expression softens. "Sometimes I forget you're an adult."

"I feel the same way about you."

"I couldn't ask for a better son."

"Okay," I say, rolling my eyes.

"I'm serious," she says. "Someday you'll understand."

The other thing everyone says.

"One question," I say, with the door slightly open.

"Shoot," she says.

"Were you ever in love?"

"Of course," she says, too quickly for it to be full of shit. "But love doesn't keep people together."

She looks away. I can see her reflection in the window, a somber expression on her face.

"I'm glad you met Tim," I say.

She turns to me, the look of sadness replaced by surprise. "Me too."

"But I'm not gonna go fishing with him."

She smiles. "I think I'm okay with that."

Outside of O'Reilly's, I take a deep breath and open the door. It's darker than I remember it. The magic of O'Reilly's is that it can change based on your mood. This time, I barely notice the statues of dragons and happy Buddhas; instead, I lose myself in the gaze of the green taxidermied cow next to the hostess stand, its insides opened for the world to see. Staring at that cow, I feel the connection that binds all life, even the kind that decides it would be a good idea to put a stuffed cow on display in a restaurant. In its eyes I see a quiet bravery, as it's forced to stand, day after day, and watch people eat its relatives. It seems to me, on the scale of terrible fates, to be at least in the top three, maybe only behind getting eaten by a shark or being named after the city your parents conceived you in.

The fortune cookie T-shirts now take on an ominous tone. The bartender rushing back and forth to refill drinks is wearing one that reads: *You learn from your mistakes . . .* When he turns around, I see the prophetic punch line: *You will learn a lot today.* A gangly kid with acne, his shirt stained with ketchup and teriyaki sauce, wears one displaying the annoying cliché *Everything happens for a reason.*

I walk over to the hostess, someone whom I vaguely recognize from my life as an actual teenager, and ask her if she's seen my dad.

"I don't know your dad," she says.

I'm pretty nervous, so I can't say I'm exactly thinking straight.

"Did you see a dad?" I correct myself, the words stumbling over one another.

"Let me check," she says.

"That's okay." I have the urge to leave the restaurant, flee the scene and head home. But it's too late.

"Ray?" I hear the familiar voice say.

I turn around, not knowing what to expect. Maybe he'd grown his hair long like he did in high school, maybe he'd shaved his head and become a monk, maybe he'd gone completely gray (maybe I should stop visualizing people only by their hairstyle).

"Dad?"

He stands in the dim light with his back to the door, the rush of cold air announcing his arrival. His hair is combed in the same direction as always, maybe a little thinner at the top, but other than that it's the same. He's put on a little weight, grown a goatee, and I've never seen him so tanned. He has the vibe of a Florida retiree, minus the Hawaiian shirt. And walker.

It's weird, but he looks more like himself.

"I can't believe I'm here," he says.

An awkward pause as I try to decipher the meaning behind his words.

"I mean in O'Reilly's," he adds quickly. "Me and my friends used to hang out here all the time."

I stand there with a glazed expression, not all that different from the stuffed cow to my left.

"We've got a lot to catch up on," he says.

The hostess intervenes just in time. "Two?"

"I found him," I say to the hostess and immediately regret it. It sounds like cheesy movie dialogue, the double meaning, the subtle undertone of a son finding his father. Yuck.

The hostess leads us to a booth in the back of the restaurant like we're the important family in a mob movie. In reality, it's the only booth not taken because it's right across from the bathroom. Best seat in the house if you have a weak bladder; not so great if you enjoy eating your meals away from people shitting.

"You're taller," my dad says as we take our seats.

"I went through puberty," I say.

My dad clears his throat and motions for the waiter. "So what's new with you?"

Too much to say. "Nothing," I answer. "You?"

The waiter comes over and takes our drink order, a pleasant interruption to our father-and-son small talk.

"Florida is hot," my dad says after the waiter leaves.

"Be careful in the sun," I say. Oh god, we've entered into talk about the weather after only five minutes. I don't know if there's enough small talk to keep us going for a whole dinner.

"I know you're going through a tough time," he says. He lets out a deep breath, as if he's relieved himself of a great burden. The toilet flushes loudly.

A tough time. He doesn't know the half of it, and I'm sure as hell not going to fill him in.

Thankfully, the waiter returns. He clumsily puts down the drinks.

"You can talk to me," my dad says quietly. He takes a sip of his beer and wipes the foam off his mustache.

"You folks ready to order?" the waiter asks, searching for his notepad.

"You ready?" my dad says.

The conversation stays on pause as we order our food. I get the Sesame Chicken Burger and my dad goes with the Orange You Glad It's Not Meat Chicken, in case you're interested, which probably depends on how hungry you are at this very moment.

"I'm trying to watch my weight," he says, cupping his stomach.

The waiter walks away and my dad resumes his obligatory father-son heart-to-heart.

"I'm sorry I haven't been around," he says, his voice stripped of all the phony airs he'd walked in with. The cheery tone that made it seem like we were at a high school reunion. He looks around the room as if we're discussing an important business deal and some-one might overhear us.

"It's fine," I say, taking a sip of my root beer.

"I wanted to give you both space."

I nod.

"That's what *you* wanted too." It feels almost accusing.

I nod again.

"You and your mom will always be important to me."

I pick my head up from my drink. It feels weird to be put in the same category as my mom, as if we're both old photographs pasted down in the same album.

The hum from the bar grows louder as more and more people show up. The steady rise in voices makes me feel calm, like no matter what happens, I'm not alone.

We sit in silence for a couple of minutes while we wait for our food, doing the awkward head bob, focusing our attention on every random object in the bar.

I think about all the questions I could ask him. The ones that would make us feel like a real father and son again. When did you first know you loved Mom? Advice about girls. Talk about all the history he's missed—the stories I'd uncovered in his absence. Instead, I keep my head down, tracing the patterns in the shiny lacquer on the table.

Maybe this is cynical, but I get the feeling that his visit is more for his conscience than it is for me. Like I've forced him to take a break from his real life and journey back into the bowels of

Burgerville. And now here we are, having dinner next to a toilet.

By the time our food comes, we're all small-talked out. I think about what he said before: *That's what you wanted.* I start to get angry. It strikes me as immature. He made the choice to move far away. A real dad would have sucked it up, rented an apartment in Murphy, and accepted the consequences—*Whatever can go wrong, will go wrong.*

By the end of dinner, I can tell my dad feels relieved. He's fulfilled his role as a dad, at least on paper, and I think that's what he came for. He's checking off the boxes so he seems like a good guy. He can play the part of the tragic hero fleeing an unhappy marriage. Respecting the wishes of his wife and son to give them space. And then flying back to his hometown to help his son cope with his demons. How brave. Fucking father of the year.

But that doesn't make his story true. Just like we used to fill in gaps about the lost history of Burgerville's unsung heroes, we're shading and coloring our own history. Only his picture looks a lot different than mine.

When we get up to leave, there's an air of finality, as if years will go by before we see each other again.

"Take care of your mom," he says.

"You too," I say. It's a habit, saying "You too" to empty gestures. Which makes me feel a little awkward because Grandma has been dead for years and he obviously won't speak to my mom.

"You sure you're okay?" he asks.

"Fantastic."

"And after everything with this girl Jane?"

I put my hand up. "I'm fine."

"Call me if you need to talk," he says. All the weight of lyrics from a pop song.

We shake hands and walk outside to where my mom is waiting for me in the parking lot. My dad waves to her, but she keeps staring straight ahead, as if he's a ghost only I can see.

83–52 DAYS BEFORE

BURGERVILLE BILL

That spring, after Jane told me she was seeing a therapist and taking medication, there was plenty of evidence that, against all odds, Simon's Law was winning out:

Exhibit A: Jane actually started trying in biology. "Wait, how does Spider-Man relate to cellular respiration?" she asked me during one of our study sessions at the library.

"I don't think Mr. Parker even knows."

"What good is a boyfriend if he can't do my homework for me?" Jane said.

Later that day, she drew a *Spider-Ma*n–esque comic featuring me trapped in a web waiting to be devoured by a spider that I could only assume was Jane—it was wearing a T-shirt that said *Let's Folk*.

Exhibit B: I'd somehow become a B student. From listening to my mom brag about me, you would have thought I'd cured cancer *and* singlehandedly dismantled a nuclear reactor.

Exhibit C: Jane was actually sleeping. Instead of texts at three a.m. about the Yeti and mind control in the CIA, we'd say good night, love you, and occasionally attempt to sext, which consisted mostly of pictures of fruit.

Exhibit D: Simon's parents bought his little brothers a trampoline, which meant another wish had come true from Delaney's wishing well. "Maybe I should have wished to end world hunger," Simon said, sounding guilty. "Well, I can't take it back. All I can do now is bounce on that thing with all my heart."

Anything that can go right, *will* go right.

One day, when walking—and maybe doing other things—in the Lost Woods, Jane and I even had our own encounter with the Flying Possum of Williamsburg. Sort of.

On the way back to Jane's house, her phone buzzed. When she looked at the screen, she screamed.

"What is it?"

"Somebody just posted something about the Flying Possum of Williamsburg," she said. "Ellie and I have had a news alert on it."

Scrolling through the search results, we saw that the Flying Possum of Williamsburg had been added to an online encyclopedia of government conspiracy theories, along with an article about a recent sighting: "It had these bat-like wings and was at least twice the size of a normal possum. The weird thing is, once I pretended to be unconscious, it just flew away." The article ended with a warning to "play possum" whenever threatened by the terrifying marsupial.

"We actually did it," Jane said.

"Maybe it's a sign that you should call Ellie," I said. I figured they had some big fight and weren't talking anymore. I thought maybe it was a chance to bring them back together.

Jane didn't say anything. Instead, she hugged me. Pulled me close to her and didn't let go for a while. I still didn't understand why an article on the internet about the Flying Possum of Williamsburg was such a big deal, but I went along with it because I loved seeing Jane happy. Even if it was because of a pretend flying rodent.

A little while later, it was the Burgerville Annual Spring Festival, the second-to-last spot on our tour of the History of Burgerville. The list remained safely in my desk drawer, where I'd put all of my Jane memorabilia. By then, though, the history of Jane and Ray had become far more important than any list or tour of Burgerville.

"We still haven't gone to Green Cow Acres," Jane said on the way over to the festival.

"You know I'm saving that spot for last."

"Works for me," Jane said, looking out the window at Burgerville's scenery—green fields, dilapidated barns, the occasional cow. "Hopefully by then, I'll be at least ninety-nine percent sure you're not a serial killer."

"I feel the same way about you," I said.

The Burgerville Annual Spring Festival dates back to the late nineteenth century. Jealous of all the attention Punxsutawney, Pennsylvania, was getting, the mayor of Burgerville came up with a festival that would rival Groundhog Day. Instead of predicting how many more weeks of winter there will be, though, our festival predicts whether or not it will be a rainy spring. And in

I smiled. "It's statements like those that make me realize why I love you so much."

We took a seat at the front of the crowd, Simon and Mary spreading out a blanket and placing a picnic basket in the center.

"Hope you're hungry," Simon said. He opened the basket, revealing a feast of every possible form of dairy: a bunch of different types of cheese, a bottle of chocolate milk, some yogurt, and something Simon called "Baked Milk," which was apparently an Eastern European delicacy.

"I think I'm becoming lactose intolerant," Mary said.

"Don't let the lactose win," Simon said.

A little while later, we saw Jane's parents. For some reason, Mr. Doe was wearing a cowboy hat. They stopped at the opposite end of the field. Mrs. Doe sat down on a lawn chair next to Mr. Doe and took out some food.

"I can't believe my dad's wearing that hat," Jane said.

"I think it looks cool."

"I love your dad's hat," Simon said, unaware of what we were talking about.

"You would," Jane said.

Then my mom showed up, holding hands with Tim.

Simon was the first to spot him. "It's a bird, it's a plane . . . No, it's Tim, Burgerville's own Superman."

There we were, the four of us, brought together by some force outside of our control, the various satellites of our lives twirling and spinning around us, as we waited to see humans misplace their faith in the power of fate, this time with the weather.

"Did you expect Burgerville to be this strange when you moved here?" Mary said to Jane. A woman with a Burgerville Bill souvenir blindfold stumbled past.

"I was pleasantly surprised," Jane said.

The announcer, dressed in head-to-toe Burgerville Bill regalia, got on the microphone. "Who's ready for Burgerville Bill?" he yelled.

A hush settled over the park. A light breeze shook the trees. Then, as if he had appeared out of thin air, Burgerville Bill began walking from the other side of the field. The crowd went wild. Women over seventy began fanning themselves.

"That man's a god," Simon said.

Bill walked to the center of the field and held up his cane. The crowd cheered like Rome celebrating the emperor. The announcer gave him the microphone.

Lester Martin had the look of an aging rock star. In spite of his age, he dressed like a kid, wearing bright blue sneakers and a faded orange shirt, his title prominently displayed in the center.

"This is my twentieth and final year doing the walk," he said. "When I was but a child, a Bill came to my second-grade class and explained the great responsibility of being a Bill, and why we must honor it. Why, no matter what happens, we must walk."

The crowd applauded.

"Who's ready to spin Burgerville Bill?" the announcer shouted into the microphone. "On the count of three . . ." Lester held up his blindfold and put it on. "One!"

Lester gave the thumbs-up.

"Two!"

He tried to touch his toes but got stuck at his knees.

"Three!"

The announcer spun Lester ten times, taking hold of his cane and giving him his arm to hold on to. Lester got his bearings and started to hobble north toward a year of good luck. "He hasn't gone north in ten years!" Simon said.

He gave me a look that said *Told you so*—more proof that Simon's Law was winning out.

But at the last second, Lester veered east and started walking to the woods.

The rules of the festival required everyone to stay completely silent so as not to influence Bill. Nobody said a word as he continued the slow march to the woods and a rainy couple of months. Good for the farmers and foliage of Burgerville, bad for everyone else.

It felt like an eternity, Bill walking with his cane, a couple steps at a time before having to catch his breath, the announcer following closely behind like a vulture stalking his prey.

"This sucks," Jane said. "I'm so tired of rain."

There was something so genuine about the way she said it, like she really thought Burgerville Bill had the power to change the weather.

And then a thought dawned on me. To this day, I don't know what came over me, but when he was about halfway to the woods, I stood up and yelled:

"You're going the wrong way!"

A thousand heads turned toward me.

"What are you doing?" Simon whispered.

"Why should we leave it to chance?" I said.

Burgerville Bill stopped dead in his tracks, disoriented.

Then I heard another voice. It was Jane's.

"Turn around!" she yelled.

Now it was all chariots of fire, Burgerville Bill with his cane pointed west, marching one slow and painful step at a time.

Gradually, though, he picked up his pace. A few people began clapping, cheering on the old man as he made his way west, toward the center of Burgerville.

Simon and Mary stood up, urging him on. Then the whole crowd joined in, a full-scale applause as Burgerville Bill made his way toward the end of the path and a spring filled with sunshine.

"It's *you*," Simon said.

"What are you talking about?"

"You're the chosen one. The next Burgerville Bill."

"What?"

"You guided him," Simon said.

He got down on one knee, giving me the respect of a king.

"Get up," I said.

He stood up, laughing. "The next Burgerville Bill," he called out, pointing at me.

The crowd joined the cheer, drunk on the moment.

"Raymond Green, the next Burgerville Bill!"

I put out my hand to Jane. "What do you say?"

Jane put her hand in mine. "Burgerville Jill? A whole new era of gender equality."

The crowd cheered even harder. Bill stood at the finish line, his white hair blowing in the wind. He took off his blindfold and shook his fist in victory. Despite the will of the gods, Burgerville had now achieved a warm and sunny spring.

I brought Jane closer and we kissed, the crowd disappearing

as I closed my eyes. When I pulled away, Jane's eyes were still closed, just like our first kiss.

We spent the rest of the afternoon finishing off the picnic basket, Simon chugging the chocolate milk to impress Mary, Jane and me poking curiously at the "Baked Milk." Every so often, someone would come to our blanket and congratulate me on my selection as the next Burgerville Bill, even though it had yet to be approved by the town council. I made sure to introduce everyone that came up to me to my First Lady of Fate, Burgerville Jill, a role Jane actually seemed to be enjoying.

"Does this title come with any actual power?" Jane asked. "Like do I get to imprison people or eat at restaurants for free?"

"You're strictly a symbol," I said.

"Just my luck."

At one point, I looked around the crowd, saw my mom and Tim sitting close together on a blanket. I watched as Mrs. Doe took Mr. Doe's cowboy hat and put it on, nestling her face close to his for a kiss. Despite all of the horrible things that happen, there was still the possibility of happiness.

I don't know what Jane was thinking that afternoon, but I like to believe it wasn't all that different from what I was thinking: Maybe it was up to us to make our own happiness.

266 DAYS AFTER

THE BUTCHER II: THE SEQUEL

I'm disappointed to say that the town council recently rejected my selection as the next Burgerville Bill in a unanimous vote. They've already created a survey on the town website for people to nominate the next Bill, but they must not know how the internet works, because Lester Martin's hair is currently in the lead.

I've decided to throw myself into a new pursuit anyway. I'm reviving Roger Lutz's ill-fated petition to change the mural on the ceiling of Town Hall to tell the truth. Today I wrote a long letter explaining why the mural is an offense to history and the real heroes of Burgerville. I've already sent it to the *Burgerville Gazette*, the town council, the mayor, and of course, Roger Lutz. Maybe I can use my powers of history to actually make a change.

I hear a knock at the door.

"Come in," I say. Simon and Mary burst into my room.

"Your room looks . . ." Simon glances around. "Exactly the same."

"It's a museum of my life," I say. "Curated by me."

After thinking about my CAR list, I invited Simon and Mary over to watch a movie. One of Rich's little steps to help me get better. Twenty Horror Movies on the Road to Recovery or something like that.

Simon pulls a DVD out of his pocket like he's smuggling contraband. "*The Butcher Two*," he says. "He's hungrier than ever."

"We just watched the first one," Mary says. "I don't think I'll ever see food the same way."

"That's the first movie we watched with Jane," I say.

"I know," Simon says. "That's why I brought it."

I know Simon means well. It's his way of telling me how much he misses Jane, even if it's by watching a movie about a man who eats people. But watching *The Butcher* is about the last thing I want to do right now.

Simon and Mary take a seat on the beanbag in the corner of my room. I move my swivel chair in front of the TV.

The opening credits play. Ominous music that makes you wonder if the Butcher's right outside the door.

"The thing about the Butcher," Simon says, "is that he's a very relatable character."

"He's a cannibal," Mary says.

"But he had a very difficult childhood. His feelings of alienation and being an outsider are universal. Right, Ray?"

I turn my head to the beanbag. Simon has his arm around Mary, their bodies pressed close, heads only inches apart.

"Everything except all the stuff about killing and eating people," I say. A thought comes to me then and it basically destroys me. In our own little story, Jane has already played her role; her screen time is over.

The Butcher makes his first appearance on screen, prepping a casserole of uncertain origin. Mary screams.

"He's literally just cooking dinner," Simon says. "Trust me, it's gonna get a lot worse."

As the movie continues, body parts flashing across the screen in soups, lasagnas, cheesecake, and an epic scene with Jell-O, I realize the main problem with history. You can talk about. Analyze it. Dissect it. Study it. Put it in a museum. But you can never, ever, no matter how hard you try, relive it. By its very definition, it's over as soon as it happens.

Meanwhile, life moves on.

Simon laughs. Mary nestles her head against Simon's shoulder. But Jane . . .

"You okay, Ray?"

"No," I say.

"What?"

Everyone's so used to me saying I'm okay. *I'm* so used to me saying I'm okay. But something about the Butcher's bad acting makes me realize I can't keep up my own crappy performance.

"I'm not okay. Jane's gone. How would I be okay?"

"Well, I know you're not *okay*, I just meant are you okay? You know what I mean?"

Simon presses pause on the TV. It happens to be just as the Butcher is dismembering a body.

"I don't know anymore."

"Maybe *The Butcher* wasn't the best idea. How about Jenga?"

"I don't want to play Jenga."

"Monopoly?"

"No."

"Maybe chess? I don't know the rules, but I'm sure I could pick it up pretty quick."

"Games aren't gonna make me feel better." I know I'm being a dick, but for some reason I can't help it.

"Sorry, I'm just trying to—"

"Then maybe stop being so fucking happy!" I yell. I immediately put my hand over my mouth. I've never yelled at Simon before. Simon looks shocked, his face contorted into the same expression he had when I explained to him how chicken nuggets are made.

Mary takes hold of his hand and angrily glares at me.

Simon looks me in the eye. "Sometimes you act like I wasn't friends with Jane too."

"It doesn't seem like it."

"I miss the old Ray," he says.

"Me too," I say.

"Ray?" my mom says through the door. "Is everything okay?"

"Everything's fine. Isn't that what you want to hear?"

She opens the door. "Ray?"

"I said I'm fine." She stands in the doorway framed by the light from the hallway. Tim walks up behind her.

"Should we invite the whole neighborhood?" I say.

"What's going on?" Tim asks.

"We were just leaving, Mrs. Green. Good day, Superman," Simon says as he passes by Tim. Tim looks startled, almost as if his secret identity has been discovered.

I hear the stairs creak as Simon and Mary leave, the front door slamming shut.

My mom glares at me. "I know you're going through a tough time, but it's no excuse to be mean to Simon. And in front of his girlfriend?"

Tim gently touches her arm, whispers something in her ear. "I'm not yelling at him," she says. "I . . ." She glances at Tim, then back to me. "I'm just worried about you."

"*We're* worried about you," Tim says. I was beginning to lose faith in my skills as a historian. I'd judged Beddington wrong. Tim. Not even my dad and I could agree on an accurate version of events. It seemed to me that everything in life was built on all of these faulty perceptions. Remove a piece and the entire structure crumbles. Everything I thought I knew about history, about Burgerville, about Jane, was wrong.

"Take a deep breath," Tim says. "Cool off. We're downstairs if you need anything."

The door closes. I think about calling Simon, but I don't even know what I'd say.

I collapse onto my bed and spot the framed photo Tim gave me for Christmas on my dresser, practically hidden behind my spelling bee trophy. My mom must have taken it out of the trash and had it fixed. I want to scream. Memories and pictures and history are all that I have now, and that just isn't enough.

36 DAYS BEFORE

JANE'S HISTORY

With the end of the school year less than a couple of months away, Jane seemed almost excited about the prospect of summer.

"No more lectures relating biology to comic books," Jane said, daydreaming about summer vacation.

"No more meatloaf from the cafeteria," Simon said.

"Summer's looking better and better," I said.

"No, I meant that as a bad thing. I look forward to that meatloaf. I even had my mom try to re-create the recipe, but it just wasn't the same."

We were waiting outside school for first period to start. Different cliques congregated, the same way they do in movies about high school, all of the clichés present, all of them sadly true: stoners kicking a hacky sack, football players flirting with the cheerleaders—Tommy Beddington at the helm, still veiled in secrecy—the Ivy Leaguers, whose very existence hinged on their academic credentials, cramming for tests, and of course, Simon, Jane and me, a category all our own.

Beddington, standing in the center of the football players, waved to us. We waved back. I thought about that night at his house when I'd become a one-man demolition crew. How getting to Jane seemed to be the most important thing in the world. Ever.

"Are you guys still undefeated in badminton?" Simon asked.

Jane was leaning against the wall, using her backpack as a cushion. "Yup. I guess it's the only game Mr. Whitley knows the rules to." She looked around the courtyard. "Does it seem like people are staring at us?"

"I always feel like that," Simon said.

"No, seriously."

I scanned the courtyard, watching everyone in their own self-absorbed little bubble, the same as always. "I think you're being paranoid," I said.

The bell rang and we ran off to our classes. Six hours until freedom.

That day, everything seemed fine. Math was the usual hour-long nap, with Mrs. Klein's soothing voice lulling me to sleep with talk of quadratic equations. During second period, Jane and I traded notes in biology as Mr. Parker attempted to teach the differences between reptiles and amphibians through characters in the Marvel Universe. The hallways contained the same slow-moving crowds, kids marching from class to class with gigantic backpacks. In American history, Jennifer Robinson continued to mix up important historical figures, asking the thought-provoking question "Did Lee Harvey Oswald really assassinate Richard Nixon?"

I guess it was wishful thinking, a case of seeing what I wanted to see, because later that day, during lunch, Tommy Beddington took a seat across from Simon and me with a grave look on his face. Jane had a different lunch that day because of her English class, and

Mary was working overtime to prepare for her first role actually playing a sentient being (a horse).

To be honest, when he first sat down, I kind of felt honored, proud in a way. Simon and I had changed so much since Jane entered the picture that Tommy Beddington could sit with us and no one would even bat an eye.

"Have you guys seen Jane?" he asked. He was staring down at his phone, his thumbs moving furiously across the screen.

Simon was still practicing the silent treatment, his own version of revenge for the years of torture and neglect. "Why?" I asked.

"It's just that . . ." He stopped typing and looked at me.

"What?"

"What'd you do to her, Beddington?" Simon said, practically foaming at the mouth.

"I didn't do anything." Tommy looked around the cafeteria, sizing up the Burgerville student body. "They know about Ellie."

"Know what?" I said. "What are you talking about?"

Tommy looked at me, squinting. "I thought she told you," he said.

"Ray, what's going on?" Simon said.

"I don't know, Simon," I said, my voice slightly raised as I angrily glared at Tommy.

He once again glanced down at his phone. After typing in a few words, he slid the phone across the table. The screen was frozen on a picture of Ellie, one half of the same photo Jane had shown me all those months ago in the McCallen Mansion.

I scrolled down and quickly scanned the article, each word like a punch in the gut, a reminder that Jane didn't trust me with her history. Simon leaned over me, his hand on my shoulder, tightening his grip as we read. The article didn't specifically name Jane, but it talked about a friend with a house on a lake in Pennsylvania. A friend who took Ellie to a steep cliff on the edge of the water. And later, a friend who had to run to get help when Ellie slipped off and hit her head on a rock. Phrases like "head trauma," "accident," and "tragedy" were sprinkled throughout the article.

"How'd you find this?" I asked, my anger dissipating into a fog of confusion.

"Laura's cousin went to school with Jane in Brooklyn. And you know how Laura is."

"Doesn't she have anything better to do?" I said.

Laura Russell, Burgerville's social media maven, lived to spread news about people, a sort of cruel personal historian.

As the lunch room filled up, the hum of conversation felt almost suffocating. "There's something else," Tommy said, practically whispering. "They also know about . . ." He glanced from side to side, his gold chain dangling in front of his chest.

His voice became quieter. "Laura's also been telling everyone about . . ."

He didn't have to finish the sentence.

"What?" Simon said, looking back and forth from Tommy to me. "I feel like I'm having dinner with my parents when they talk about the economy."

I didn't have the heart to say it. It just didn't feel right to talk about Jane's wrist in the middle of the cafeteria. I heard a low murmur of whispers. "It's none of anyone's business," I said, suddenly furious at the entire lunch room, the kids craning their necks to hear the latest news.

I stood up. I could feel everybody's eyes on me. "Don't you have anything better to do?" I screamed.

"Take it easy, man," Tommy said.

"You're scaring the lunch ladies," Simon said.

Most people had stopped their conversations and were staring right at us.

I looked back at Simon and Tommy. "We've gotta find her." Simon and Tommy slowly got up, as if trying to slip out unnoticed. We made our way out of the cafeteria, our shoes squeaking on the floor, the metallic clang of the door opening, the dim of the hallway. It was agreed that Simon and Tommy would split up and search the school, while I'd take the Red Rocket and look around Burgerville.

But as I was running through the hallway to the exit, Jane's whereabouts came to me with a certainty I still can't quite explain.

On the way to Beddington's statue, I tried to plan what I'd say. I was sad about Ellie, upset that Jane felt like she had to keep this part of her life a secret. But I was also mad at her for telling Tommy Beddington and not me.

I found her with her back to the stone pedestal. Her forehead rested on her knees. Dwarfed by Beddington, she looked like a small child.

"I guess you know," she said. She remained staring at the ground.

I texted Simon, told him to find Tommy and let him know Jane was okay.

I sat down next to her and hugged her. Her body remained stiff. "Darth Vader not wearing any pants," I said.

"Mr. Parker dressed as Darth Vader not wearing any pants," Jane said, her voice muffled.

"Once again, too realistic," I said.

She picked her head up and let out a quiet laugh.

"Why didn't you tell me?" I asked.

Jane shrugged.

"Seriously," I said, getting worked up, as if her omission was somehow an indication of our love for each other—or lack thereof. "I can't believe you told Tommy Beddington and not me."

Jane kept her gaze focused on the horizon. "That's what you're upset about?"

"I don't know. I mean, you're supposed to tell me that kind of stuff."

"I get to choose how I tell my story, right?"

She turned to me.

"Jane, I don't want some pretend perfect version of you. You can tell me things."

She scoffed and shook her head.

"What?"

"I watched my best friend die," she said. "Okay?"

"I know. It's horrible. I can't even imagine what that's like. Roger Lutz says—"

"I swear if you tell me something else about history I'm gonna lose it."

I stopped cold. "I'm just trying to help—and you don't make that easy. Nothing's easy with you."

"What's that supposed to mean?"

"I'm always either trying to cheer you up or say the right thing or not say the wrong thing. It can be exhausting."

"Dating me sounds like a real hassle," she said.

"That's not what I'm saying. You're the best thing that ever happened to me. But *you* have to realize that." I thought back to the two of us shouting at Burgerville Bill, taking fate into our own hands. "We can make our own happiness."

"That's great for us," Jane said. "But Ellie never had that chance. And it's all my fault."

"What are you talking about?"

She spoke softly. Wouldn't look at me. Picked at her nails until her fingers started bleeding. She told me it was her idea to sneak out that night. That she was the one who convinced Ellie to join her on the edge of the lake. That somehow, all of this sadness led back to her.

She took a deep breath and exhaled.

"After Ellie died, I had this voice in my head. The images of Ellie falling, staring right at me. I couldn't make it stop."

"Is that when you . . ."

She glanced down at her wrist. "I thought people would be better off."

"Don't say that," I said. I pulled her close to me, felt myself come undone as she cried; quietly at first, until her whole body started shaking.

We sat there without talking, shielding our eyes from the sun as it began its downward trek. I thought about perspective. How the sun appeared to be moving even though it was the earth spinning. An understanding based on faulty reasoning could change how you saw the world.

As I stared off into the distance trying to find the right thing to say, I noticed a penny on the ground, flickering in the sun. I picked it up and held it between my thumb and index finger, looking at it as if it held all of the answers to Jane's questions, as if it could explain everything I couldn't. I carefully placed it in her palm.

"You never told me what you wished for," I said. "Right now we're two out of three."

Jane sat up straight and held the coin in front of her eyes. After a few seconds, she threw it over her shoulder with a flick of her wrist, the way you'd shoo away a bug or get rid of something too hot to touch. "I wished for something impossible," she said. The coin clanged on the pavement and rolled to the grass. "I know better now."

When Jane was ready to leave, I led her to the Red Rocket, wishing we could take off, leave Burgerville, leave Earth.

Instead, we drove around until the end of school, Jane barely speaking, her forehead pressed against the window as we made loops around Burgerville.

35–9 DAYS BEFORE

THE OTHER WILLIAMSBURG

After Jane's old life crept back into her new life, things were different. Kids whispered about Jane's past, making her relive Ellie's death over and over again.

At Burgerville High, Jane and I became ghosts. We ate lunch together, went to school together, and when Jane was up to it, hung out. But the gaps returned. There were days when Jane wouldn't go to school. Other days, she'd refuse to see me, wouldn't even talk to me.

Of course, I took it personally. I'd call her on the phone, ask her to hang out, but she was avoiding me.

"Where were you today?"

"Home."

"Are you sick?"

"No."

"Can I come over?"

"Not today. I don't feel well."

"But you just said you weren't sick."

"I need to be alone."

"You need to be with someone."

"Don't be *that* boyfriend."

"I'm worried about you."

"I'm fine. Go hang out with Simon."

It got so bad that I called her parents.

"Ray?" Mrs. Doe said into the phone.

"I'm worried about Jane."

I told them about what happened at school, how everyone knew about Ellie and about how Jane had tried to kill herself. I didn't know what else to do.

"Jane told us," Mrs. Doe said. I heard her sigh.

"We'll have her see her therapist more," Mr. Doe said.

"Please keep an eye on her, Ray," Mrs. Doe said, speaking over Mr. Doe.

"We've been through this before," Mr. Doe said, his voice sounding tired.

"We were hoping Burgerville would be a fresh start," Mrs. Doe said.

"She just needs time," Mr. Doe said.

Simon felt the same.

"You have to give her space," he said.

"How much?"

"As much as she needs. Jane is like a cat. You have to wait for her to come to you." He paused. "And she can jump really high."

But I worried that the more space I gave her, the more likely she'd go spiraling out on her own. I waited and waited and waited, until a couple of weeks later, Jane called me—I practically jumped when I saw her name on the caller ID—and asked me to drive her to Brooklyn to see her old neighborhood. I felt funny about it, especially since reminders of Ellie seemed to make her so sad, but I would've done anything just to see Jane at that point, so I agreed.

Instead of lying to my mom about why I needed the car, I figured I'd just tell her, though I did wait to ask until Tim was around. Regardless of my mixed feelings about him, he seemed to have a calming effect on the whole house.

At first, she shook her head, crossed her arms, and gave a definitive "Absolutely not."

"Hear me out," I said. "I've been driving for over a year, we're only going to Brooklyn, and we'll go on a Saturday, when there's not as much traffic."

"I'm sorry, Ray, there's no way I'm letting you drive Jane to Brooklyn. I can't believe the Does are okay with this."

"It's important for her to visit her old neighborhood," I said.

"Why?" my mom asked.

"Why do you look through old photo albums?"

I looked at Tim to gauge his reaction. I always wondered how he felt about my mom's other existence, her life being married to my dad.

"Sometimes I visit my hometown," Tim said. "When I need a little perspective."

"You're from Centerville," my mom said. "A few miles away."

"You can't help where you're born," Tim said.

"So you think I should let him go?"

It was an innocent question, but it was the type of thing she might have asked my dad.

My mom's face reddened, as if she was having the same thought.

"It's up to you," Tim said. He squeezed her hand.

"Okay," she said after a while. "Fine. But you've got to be back before dinner."

Maybe I was onto something with this whole acting mature thing after all.

"Thanks, Mom," I said.

"Just be safe," she said.

"I think you've earned a hug."

She looked surprised.

"What?" I said. "It's not like I'm taking any AP courses next year."

"Just come here," she said.

On the drive to Brooklyn, Jane stared out the window as the skyline of New York City took shape in the distance. The traffic thickened, speeding up and slowing down, an incomprehensible rhythm I couldn't seem to get a handle on. Taking the train to New York was one thing, but driving there felt like a constant assault.

"You're sure you want to do this?"

"I don't know."

"We can still turn back. Take a trip to Green Cow Acres."

"Not today," she said.

We sped up as the traffic thinned and drove down FDR Drive. I remained hyper alert as cars honked their horns and sped in front of me.

"Before we go to Williamsburg, there's something I want to show you."

Jane guided me off the highway, right into the chaotic streets of Manhattan. I had no idea where I was going, but Jane seemed to know the neighborhood as well as I knew Burgerville, pointing out famous delis, parks she used to go to, a spot Ellie claimed was a Cold War–era testing facility for remote viewing.

We finally parked in the middle of a deserted block. Graffiti spotted the walls—tag names and figures drawn in silhouette beneath awnings announcing live music and used guitars for sale. Coffee shops and bars scattered in between.

Jane got out of the car, scanning the block. She shut the door and hesitantly began walking down the street. I followed, our shoulders lightly touching as we walked.

"Ellie and I would hang out here for hours on the weekends," Jane said quietly. "Buying CDs, T-shirts, the occasional joint. There's a whole underground folk music scene." She had this far-away look on her face, like she could see the tie-dye and hear the gentle strumming of acoustic guitar.

"What was she like?" It was the first time I'd ever directly asked.

Jane looked caught off guard. She took a deep breath and exhaled. "She was funny. I wish you could have heard her tell the backstory of the Flying Possum of Williamsburg. It was epic."

We walked faster.

"She liked mysteries. She was always finding some crazy place to explore. A weird story to research. I guess it made things not feel so . . ."

"True?"

She smiled. "Exactly. And she believed in stuff. The random conspiracy theories, but other things too. Dogs. The feeling you get in your stomach when you ride a roller coaster. The first day of a new school year. Me."

She took my hand, pulling me along. "Just a little bit farther."

We were practically jogging by the time we stopped in front of a store called Irene's. "Here we are," Jane said, out of breath.

"You mean?"

Jane nodded. "Now it's mostly a grocery store, but back in the sixties, it used to be one of the best folk venues in the whole country. It's where my grandma got her start. One of her fans bought it and named it after her."

As we walked through the door, a prerecorded guitar strummed a happy chord. In between the narrow aisles, I could see an acoustic guitar propped up on a small stage in the back. Signs hung on the walls, advertising various shows that had taken place there over the years. Bands like Tambourine Jamboree and Neon Rainbow and a mysterious woman with the moniker Mother Folker.

"They sometimes have shows at night," Jane said. "There's nothing like grocery shopping while listening to folk music."

Next to the stage, there was a poster of a young Grandma Irene above a tattered piece of paper outlining her contributions to the world of folk music. She had an acoustic guitar strapped around her body and was wearing a tie-dye headband. Her nails were painted all different colors. Just like Jane's.

"That's her before the Folk Williamsburg Festival," Jane said. "Before my grandparents and my mom left Burgerville. That's how I like to remember her." She paused, bowed her head, like she was saying a prayer.

As we were leaving, the man at the counter called out to Jane. His movements were slow, like a wind-up toy running out of power. He had tufts of white hair sprouting from his ears and nose, though it was conspicuously absent from his head. "I thought I recognized you," he said.

"Hi, Mr. Palmer."

"Still listening to your grandma's music?" the man said. "She was quite the singer."

"Every day," Jane said.

"I still remember her first show," he said. "Watched her play just a few feet from where you're standing."

"I wish I could have been there," Jane said.

"You play any folk?"

"Me?" Jane's tone made it sound like he'd asked her if she'd ever been to Mars.

"Yes, you. Music's in your blood."

Jane shook her head. "I think it skipped a couple generations."

"You can't escape your genes," he said.

I put my arm around Jane and we walked out of the store, a happy chord playing as we left.

On the ride to Williamsburg, neither of us spoke. We crossed silently over the bridge, watching the current of the East River move steadily below, water shimmering in some spots, a brownish hue closer to shore.

Once we made it over the bridge, Jane directed me through the streets of Williamsburg, until she told me to park along a quiet side street, the hum of the city barely audible.

"My old street," Jane said. A smile brushed her lips before quickly retreating.

It was a row of faded brick buildings, the tops almost castle-like, a row of teeth extending out of the brick. Metal fire escapes were placed haphazardly along the front, staircases without a clear end or beginning, similar to a design you might see in an Edward

P. Delaney blueprint. Ivy grew in patches on the brick; in some places it appeared to be spreading, on the verge of covering the windows and doors. Trees lined the sidewalks, angrily jutting up from beneath the concrete. Surprisingly, there was no sign of tight pants or flannel or eighteenth-century beards.

After a few minutes of sitting in silence, Jane opened the car door. She walked quickly, head down, determined, the way some-one looks when they're marching into a storm. I followed. She finally paused in front of a building with a ramp that ran parallel to the front, leading to an entryway framed by a green awning.

"My dad would never let anyone push him," Jane said, making her way up the ramp.

"Oh" was all I could muster.

"One time the power went out and he couldn't get upstairs. He had to go wait at a restaurant across the street."

"It wasn't your fault," I said. "It was an accident."

"I thought everything in history has a reason. A cause."

"It does. But that doesn't mean it's you."

"Whatever." Jane sighed, grabbed hold of the railing, and tilted her head back to look at a window a few stories up. She shook her head and marched away.

Once we got off Jane's street, thick crowds stampeded along the sidewalk, most people with headphones in their ears, looking down at their cellphones. The sun shone brightly, blazing on the asphalt.

"Where are you going?" I asked her.

"I want to show you one last thing."

People splintered around us. Jane and I were in our own orbit once again. I had the feeling that we could deflect anything that came our way if we just stayed together.

Jane walked ahead. She stopped in front of a black wrought-iron gate. Behind it, there was a small park filled with flowers. There were four benches arranged around the center. She walked through the gate and stopped in front of one of the benches.

I walked beside her. After a few seconds, I realized she was looking at something: a small inscription on a gold-plated plaque, barely visible: *Eleanor _____: 1999–2015.*

"So much for history," Jane said.

Somehow, I knew what she meant. At least I think I did. The past year I'd been telling her stories about wacky mayors, Burger-ville Bill, Earl Beddington and the green cows. But that's all they were: stories. Monuments to the past. A bench in the middle of the park reminding the world that a girl named Ellie had lived in the other Williamsburg. So much for history.

"She went to college out west," Jane said. "She studied fossils." She shrugged, as if saying it surprised even her. "But not dino-saurs or anything like that. Something completely random, like an ancient species of kangaroo that used to hop all around North America until the meteor hit."

I assumed she'd gone insane. Then I realized what she was doing. She was telling Ellie's story. Writing a history that could never actually be.

"After discovering a gigantic species of kangaroo," I continued, "she was awarded the Australian Nobel Peace Prize."

"But she donated all the money to charity."

"Her favorite charity," I added, "an organization focused on fighting the scourge that is awkward conversations with people in elevators."

"That's when she met her husband, a prince from some small country in Europe with a lot of syllables."

"At a fundraiser?"

"In the elevator," Jane said, "while doing fieldwork. And the wedding wasn't one of those super-stuffy ceremonies where the bride and groom profess their love to each other in front of a hundred strangers. They got married . . ." Jane scrunched up her forehead. "In Burgerville. In front of Earl Beddington himself. God, Ellie would have loved Burgerville."

I hugged her. Kissed her. Tried to make her forget, or remember, I wasn't sure which. We sat there for a while, the many possibilities of Ellie's life hovering over us, each of those futures now nothing more than wishes.

8 DAYS–1 DAY BEFORE

THE LAST DAY

After that day, things changed pretty quickly. I can roughly sketch the outline, the facts, the what, but I still can't put them together in a way that makes sense.

I imagine Jane in her room, staring at the ceiling while the phone rang, while her parents knocked on the door, while I spoke to them at the bottom of the stairs in hushed whispers, Mr. Doe and Mrs. Doe trying to remain upbeat, like they had everything under control. She was trying a new medicine, seeing her therapist twice a week, doing yoga once in a while, even considering taking up folk guitar.

I'd wake up panicked in the middle of the night, thinking about her wrist, the raised skin, rough to the touch.

"You have to respect her space," my mom told me when I asked her for advice.

"I don't want her to think I forgot about her," I said.

"Jane needs more than a boyfriend right now," she said.

So I started researching how I could help, even read through all of McCallen's therapy techniques, before realizing they'd probably been updated, as most of them involved a padded cell.

I ransacked my mom's library for self-help books, trying to find clues and ideas. I became a walking encyclopedia of breathing techniques, mantras, relationship advice.

I'd drop off books, talk to her parents, call Jane up and ask her if she tried various breathing techniques.

"Have you tried the three-two-one breathing release?"

"Yup."

"And?"

"I'm a little out of breath."

Or visualization:

"You're flying through space surrounded by light."

"I'm in my bed under the covers."

"You're missing the point."

Or even the law of attraction:

"Why don't you cut out pictures of various things you want to achieve? Places you want to go."

"You want me to make a fucking collage?" she said.

"Fine, how about this. Think about . . ." I tried to come up with something good, but everything I thought of seemed stupid. A dog with lobster claws? More variations on Mr. Parker in strange and somewhat disturbing outfits? Mythical creatures doing everyday household activities? "Just think about a platypus," I finally said. "Nature's own random image."

"It's not working," she said. She sounded withdrawn. Like she was talking from another dimension.

I continued calling, but she'd always have an excuse. "I'm tired," she'd say, or "It's getting late," or "I just need to sleep it off."

No matter the strategy, Jane didn't seem to respond. She stayed in her room, listening to folk records while the rest of the world marched on.

After an entire week of Jane refusing to see me, she showed up unexpectedly at my house, just like her first appearance all those months ago for our Never Have I Ever game.

The Jane that stood at the bottom of the steps wasn't the Jane of the Burgerville Spring Festival. Her mouth curled almost imperceptibly when she saw me, the sinister smile struggling to assert itself. She had on sweatpants and a T-shirt Simon had made for her that said *Burgerville Jill*. It looked too big for her, like she was drowning in Burgerville apparel.

"Hi," she said when I reached the bottom of the stairs.

"Hi," I said.

"Ta-da." I wanted to hug her, hold her tighter and tighter.

"I've been so worried about you."

"Sorry," she said.

"Don't be sorry." She kind of fell into me, like she couldn't hold herself up. "I've got a bunch of new activities for you to try," I said.

She sighed. "Please no more imagining myself in a pool of cheese."

We walked upstairs and went to my room, the floor littered with my mom's self-help books, McCallen's biography, other history volumes from our tour of Burgerville scattered in between.

"I'm sorry I've been such a bummer lately," she said.

"I've missed you," I said.

"I miss you too."

She looked down at her hands. No color on her nails. The bracelets were gone. The scar on full display. "I'm just trying to figure things out."

"If you want to be happy, be happy," I said, channeling Grandma Irene, trying to cheer Jane up.

"I wish things were that simple," she said. "There's something in my head. I mean, it sounds like I'm saying I'm possessed or something, but that's how it feels. I get sad. Then I get mad at myself for being sad. And then I get mad at myself for getting mad at myself. It's just so much noise."

"Try this," I said. I turned on Grandma Irene's mix CD, featuring unknown classics like "Peace, Love, and Cows" and "Hippie History."

The soft acoustic played in the background, Grandma Irene practically whispering through the speakers.

"I swear, sometimes I think she's talking to me," Jane said.

We sat on the edge of my bed holding hands, just listening, letting the music work its magic. After a few songs, I heard my mom's car pull into the driveway. Jane instinctively got up from the bed and made her way to the window.

"You don't have to sneak out," I said.

Jane was already undoing the locks. "Okay." She sat back down on the edge of the bed. Grandma Irene's gentle strumming continued playing in the background as she sang about a world filled with happiness. Before Burgerville had cast her out. Before her depression had taken over.

My mom appeared outside the doorway with Tim by her side.

At first she looked like she was going to get mad. But her expression softened when she saw Jane, who I realized barely looked like herself.

"Jane's here," I said.

"I can see that," my mom said.

"Hi, Mrs. Green," Jane said. "Hi, Tim. I was just on a walk, so I thought I'd stop by."

"All the way from the New York Strip?" my mom asked.

"It helps clear my head," Jane said.

"Tim's making his famous chili," my mom said.

"It's not famous," Tim said. "A little bit of press in the food blogs, but—"

"Do you want to stay for Tim's doomed-to-obscurity chili?" I asked.

"That's not a bad name," Tim said.

"I'd like to, but I think I should be getting home," Jane said.

"You're always welcome," my mom said. She looked at me. Concern, a slight tilt of her head toward Jane. I shrugged.

"Thanks, Mrs. Green, that means a lot." She appeared to be on the verge of crying, but something stopped her from letting go.

Tim and my mom went downstairs.

"So you're okay?"

"I'm fine," Jane said.

"Jane?"

"I'm fine."

"Can I bring you home?"

"I feel like walking," she said. "I'm meeting my mom in town."

"Let me take you home," I said.

"I *need* to walk," she said.

She got up and opened the window. "Look at the moon," she said.

I joined her at the window. The moon looked like it was on the verge of falling from the sky, a gigantic glowing orb.

"I've explained Roger Lutz's theory about full moons, haven't I?"

"A few times," she said. The slightest hint of a smile.

"And?"

"It makes just as much sense as anything else."

"I guess it is a little ridiculous."

"No," Jane said. "It's not. We need people like you and Roger Lutz to look for answers."

"Kind of like a superhero historian?"

"Sort of," Jane said, "If that's what you want to tell yourself."

She kissed me and stepped out of the window onto the tree, so only her torso was visible.

"I'm having déjà vu," I said.

I thought back to the night of our Never Have I Ever game, how Jane had called me over to the window right before Simon threw up milk and cookies all over my rug. Were we meant to kiss that night? Were we meant to be, period?

I moved closer to the window.

"I just want you to know that you make me feel normal," Jane said. She kissed me. "Scrabble-on-a-Saturday-night normal."

I hugged her, my body half inside, half outside.

"Me too," I said. "Arguing-over-who-lost-the-remote-control normal."

A dark shadow moved across the yard. We both turned our attention outside just in time to see the trees at the edge of my lawn begin to sway.

"The Flying Possum of Williamsburg," I said.

Jane laughed. The last time I ever heard her laugh. "Why not?" she said.

She climbed down the tree and, hanging from a branch, lowered herself to the ground. I watched as she walked through my yard, zigzagging across the grass. I waved good-bye, even though I knew she couldn't see me.

Later, I called her to make sure she was okay. She said she was tired, she needed some rest, she was *fine*.

"I'll come over if you need me," I said.

"Ray, I'm fine."

"Fine as in fine? Or fine as in I-don't-feel-like-talking-about-my-problems fine?"

"Fine as in we're-all-spinning-a-thousand-miles-an-hour-on-a-piece-of-rock-in-the-middle-of-space-and-we're-on-our-own fine."

"Okay."

I wish there was more of an ending. An explanation. Something to point at and say *aha!* That's the reason *why*. I wish I'd called her parents that night. I wish I hadn't believed her when she said she was fine. I wish I'd made some grand gesture to the universe, a string quartet outside of her window, something better than *normal*. But in life, there's no genies, no do-overs, no second chances, no one answering your prayers. We said good night. I studied for a history test I had the next day. And sometime in the middle of the night, everything I thought I knew about Jane and the world changed.

0 DAYS BEFORE

THE UNKNOWABLE WHY

Early the next morning, my phone rang and I picked up, expecting to hear Jane on the other line.

Instead, it was her mom. "Ray?" A deep sob. Voices in the background. Quick bursts of breath.

"Mrs. Doe?" I felt my own breathing go shallow as a million thoughts raced through my head, all of them ending in the same dark place.

"Jane's gone, Ray," Mrs. Doe said in a quiet whisper.

"What are you talking about? She's back in the city?"

"Is that Ray?" Mr. Doe asked, his voice sounding far away. I heard him begin yelling, asking to speak to me.

"She's with her grandma Irene," Mrs. Doe said. She began wailing with a haunting intensity. I heard Mr. Doe's motor rumble in the background as he made his way over to her.

At that point, my knees buckled and I collapsed to the floor. I could hear the faint sound of Mr. and Mrs. Doe's voices, the words no longer registering.

It was then that I realized how stupid I was to believe in wishing wells and Simon's Law, a world where history doesn't weigh you down but somehow sets you free.

Because sometime in the middle of the night, Jane decided it made more sense to leave than to stay. She swallowed a bottle of pills and never woke up.

1 DAY–6 DAYS AFTER

GREEN COW ACRES

I can only remember fragments of the next few days. I remember going to the wake and seeing Jane's body lying in the casket. Placing the list of Burgerville sites in her hand, almost losing it when I noticed someone had painted her nails red. The funeral, where the priest assured everyone Jane was happy now, that she was with her grandma Irene. I couldn't help but roll my eyes. Just like Jane would have. Awkward conversations with the Does, where we hovered over the question of why, and for the first time talked about Jane in the past tense, as if she was now just another piece of Burgerville's history.

Everyone wanted to talk about it with me.

My mom: "I'm here for you."

Tim: "You can talk to me, Bud."

Simon: "I didn't realize something could hurt this much."

And then there were the accusing glances at school, as if I had played a part in her suicide. I needed to be alone, away from everyone, away from myself, if possible.

A few days after the funeral, I even called Roger Lutz, hoping he could give me perspective.

"Mr. Lutz moved to Florida," the woman at the Burgerville

Historical Association said. "He wanted to be closer to his family."

"Do you have his number?"

"Mr. Lutz isn't taking calls anymore."

"Is he still working on his new book?"

"Sadly, no. He's . . ." She paused. It must have been too hard to talk about his Alzheimer's. "His biography of Earl Beddington is on hold for the time being."

I put down the phone. Even Roger Lutz had abandoned me.

That night, I drove out to Green Cow Acres, the last spot on our list. It felt like an obligation to finish our tour of Burgerville, even if it meant finishing it alone. I parked my mom's car on the side of the road, stepped over the No Trespassing sign, and ran to the middle of the field.

I don't know what I was expecting. If I'd be eaten by a green cow or get some sort of message from Jane. I was fine with either.

The grass had been cut recently, part of the town council's attempt to turn Green Cow Acres into a park. After all these years, they still couldn't figure out what to do with it.

I sat down in the grass. Imagined Earl Beddington with his rag-tag mob, attempting to capture or kill the mutant cows supposedly terrorizing Burgerville. Holding his pitchfork as he waited to meet his fate. If you thought something long enough, could you trick yourself into believing it?

I asked the question that needed answering, the question I'd been taught to look for as a historian.

"Why?" I said.

The wind rustled the grass. Dark clouds moved in from the horizon.

"Why?" I shouted at the sky.

But no answers came. In that moment, I finally understood how Jane felt about Ellie. No matter what people said, nothing would change the fact that Jane was gone. Words were meaningless. When someone was gone, they were really gone.

"You took up the guitar," I found myself saying, head tilted to the sky.

The silence expanded. I could hear the faint sound of crickets, a steady buzzing, as if the world's gears were turning.

"You wrote songs like your grandma. About being happy. Moving on. The joys of a good condiment."

My eyes began to tear up, the many possibilities of Jane collapsed into a few sentences.

"After your first platinum album, we settled down in Burgerville." My voice grew quiet, like I was whispering in Jane's ear. "I finished writing Roger Lutz's history of Earl Beddington and you took some time off to . . ." I thought about Jane showing up at Beddington's statue for our first date. How grateful I was to have that memory. How grateful I was to have every memory with Jane. "You took some time off to prove the existence of Beddington's green cows," I said.

I could almost hear Jane laugh.

"We got married." I felt the words catch, as if someone had poured sand down my throat. "Simon wanted to jump out of the cake, but we had to tell him no. And it wasn't all happily ever after, but we made it work. We made our own happiness."

I stared up at the sky, not a star in sight, waiting for a response I knew would never come.

The darkness grew even darker. Thunder echoed in the

distance. I knew I should walk back to my car, but there was something exhilarating about being out there.

It started to rain. Just a few drops at first, then a full-on downpour. Still, I didn't budge. It was like the universe was testing me or something, and I wasn't going to let it win.

After a while, I almost forgot it was raining. It was like I was sitting at the bottom of the ocean floor. Fuzzy shapes in the distance. Lightning flashing across the sky. The rain, how a bunch of tiny droplets can create a single sound, a motor powered by a collective purposelessness. Cars whooshed by in the distance, their headlights barely a dent in the thick cover of night.

I suddenly remembered that this wasn't only the field of green mutant cows—it was also the field where Grandma Irene had put on her Folk Williamsburg Festival. A story left out of most of Burgerville's history books.

Another flash of lightning.

What we leave out shapes the truth, changes how we tell a story.

The rain came down even harder.

We can choose which sources to include. We can organize the chaos.

I got to my feet. Stood still as the rain and wind whipped at my neck, my face, my back. I planted my feet more firmly into the ground.

Even though our future was now only make-believe, our past was real. That's where the answers were. If anyone could put together the pieces of Jane's story in a way that made sense, it was me.

I sprinted back to the car, mud sloshing at my ankles as I swam through the wall of rain. A full moon shining overhead, only glimpsed in hazy light behind the clouds. I started the car, turned the windshield wipers on, and pressed play on Grandma Irene's CD. I drove home, my clothes drenched, blaring folk music with a single purpose in mind.

That's when I started compiling sources for *The History of Jane Doe*.

287 DAYS AFTER

ANGER

My sessions with Rich have become just one exercise after another.

"When you go home today, I want you to pick an object in your room. Any object."

"You sound like a magician," I say.

"And after you pick the object, I want you to write a paragraph about what it means to you."

"I don't think so," I say.

"Okay," Rich says, scrolling through his pad. "Then I want you to think about a memory with Jane and—"

"No," I say.

Rich nods. I can see the wheels in his head spinning as he tries to figure out how to proceed.

"Any luck with the petition?"

"We've just reached double digits," I say. "Another colossal waste of time."

"You're giving up," he says.

"I'm giving up," I repeat.

I begin to study the cracks in the ceiling to avoid Rich's gaze.

"You're not a quitter," he says.

"And you're not an exercise guru."

"What would Jane want?"

"I don't want to talk about what Jane would want," I say, looking him straight in the eye.

"Why?"

"Because I have no clue what Jane wanted."

"In my experience," Rich says, "people with Jane's type of depression are complicated."

"Wait, are you—"

He holds up his hand, as if giving me a signal, a stop sign.

"It's not about the people in their lives. Their boyfriends. Parents. Friends. It's something inside. And that's hard for people to get, because it doesn't necessarily relate to anything going on in their lives—it's just there. And sometimes, when people don't get the help they need, it grows too strong."

"So why didn't you help her?" I ask.

Rich looks at me, then down at his notepad, before finally settling on the emoji clock on the opposite wall.

"I ask myself that question every day," he says. "Hypothetically speaking, of course."

"You should have known," I say.

"Maybe," Rich says. "But can I change it? No. Do I have to accept it? Not exactly. I can reframe it by—"

"Stop with the bullshit exercises," I snap.

Rich recoils. The anger came so sudden and unexpected that I wonder if I've been momentarily possessed.

"Sorry," I say.

"Stay with your anger," he says.

"Fuck!" I yell.

"Good."

"Fuck!" I yell louder.

"Great," Rich says, "let it out."

"Mother fuck fuck fuck fuck!"

"Who are you angry at?"

"You!"

"Good," he says. "Tell me why."

" 'Cause you wear those fucking corduroys and you think you're so fucking smart."

"Keep going," he says.

"And you said you could help me, but you can't!"

"Who else are you angry at?"

"My mom," I say.

"Why?"

"Because she's dating Superman and he's just as fucking one-dimensional as the comic book character."

"Who else?"

"Tim. 'Cause I actually like him."

Rich nods.

"Now my dad," I say, completely unprompted. "Because he bailed and now wants to pretend like nothing happened. *He's* the one who moved to Florida, not me.

"And you too, Simon," I say to the chair that had once played Simon. "Fuck you for being able to move on!"

My hands are shaking, my eyes wet. "Fuck me for being dumb enough to think that I could actually figure things out."

"More," Rich says.

"And fuck you, Jane!" I scream at the ceiling. "You and your folk music, your depression, the Flying Possum of Williamsburg, your guilt, fuck it all."

Rich lets his notepad fall to the floor. I must have been wrath-of-God angry; I imagine Rich with his eyes open wide, the ceiling chipping, tiles being blown apart, water pipes breaking, a green cow flying through the air. I'm a tornado.

"And most of all, Jane, fuck you for leaving me here alone. For showing me happiness and then taking it all away."

And then the storm is spent. I collapse back into my chair. My legs go weak and I slither to the floor like a pile of clothes.

Rich kneels beside me. "I'm sorry," he says, like a mad composer who has just knowingly conducted his symphony to the brink. "I'm sorry."

"Why's she gone?" I say.

Rich doesn't respond.

"Why am I here and she's not?"

"There's no why," Rich says.

"There's *only* why," I say. My head is pounding. I want to pull all my hair out just to release the pressure.

I can't breathe. I just keep thinking of Jane. How I would never get an explanation. How I should have been there for her. I can't get enough oxygen. I can't *breathe*.

I close my eyes and that's when everything goes black.

287 DAYS AFTER, CONT'D

THE HOSPITAL

I woke up in the hospital a couple of hours ago. The doctor told me he wants to run some tests just to be safe, make sure it's nothing more serious than an anxiety attack. Which means I'm stuck in this room until tomorrow morning. The fluorescent lights are burning my eyes. Wheels screech over linoleum, an ominous sound, as if the nurses are coming to get me next.

I can hear my roommate snoring, almost like an engine running. A thin curtain separates us. From the sound of his snoring, I can predict with ninety percent accuracy that his nose has been broken multiple times and he's divorced.

My mom's passed out in the chair by the bed. She's much more pleasant now than when she first got to the hospital. It almost felt like an interrogation. *Why'd you pass out? Who do you think you are?* I guess everyone's a little on edge.

I hear a familiar voice and tense up.

"Where's Raymond Green?" the voice asks.

"Room two twenty-three."

I hear squeaky shoes and see a shadow passing the door, walking all the way to the end of the hall. Those shoes, that lack of direction, it can only mean one thing: Simon's here.

Things have been weird ever since my fight with Simon. I guess we both needed some time to process everything that happened.

He walks into the room. The snoring has only gotten louder, almost as if we have our own symphony, the swell of the snore rising with the anticipation of Simon and me coming face-to-face after a few weeks of not talking.

Something about him seems different. He looks older. More stylish. Like he's living up to his role as the son of a politician. Then he takes a couple of steps and practically brings down half the machines in the room, and I know it's the same old Simon.

"You're not going to flatline on me now, are you?"

"I should be okay." I hold up my arms, showing the lack of tubes.

"I think I found my calling," he says.

"What's that?"

"I'm becoming a doctor."

"You're inspired and you want to help people?" I ask.

"Something about the white uniforms and the smell of bleach. It reminds me of heaven."

I laugh. It feels almost like old times.

"I'm sorry about—"

Simon puts his hand up before I can finish and accidentally knocks over a glass of water. "Water under the bridge," he says. "I obviously did that on purpose."

My mom moves a little.

"What happened?" Simon says, a serious tone to his voice.

"I passed out," I say.

"I thought . . ." Simon doesn't finish his sentence. "Can I have your Jell-O?" he asks.

"Sure. How's Mary?"

"Good," he says. "Sometimes I still can't believe I have a girl-friend."

He puts his hand over his mouth.

"Sorry," he says. I'm used to this type of reaction, people editing themselves, afraid they'll say the wrong thing, somehow remind me of Jane and what I lost—what Simon and I both lost.

"It's okay."

We sit for a minute. "Do you ever think about her?" I ask.

"All the time."

The door creaks open. Both of us turn to the little sliver of light painted across the floor. It closes, darkening the room. I can tell Simon's thinking the same thing as me.

"You still believe in ghosts?" I ask.

Simon nods as if the evidence is right in front of him.

"Do you have the Red Rocket?"

Simon pulls out his keychain. A miniature dog hangs off the ring.

"What do you say we take a ride?"

Simon hesitates. "Are you supposed to leave the hospital?"

"Your dad's on the town council," I say. "You make the rules."

"At least put on some pants."

I grab my pants off the chair, pull off my hospital dressing gown, and throw on a shirt and jacket. Simon slurps the last bit of Jell-O out of the cup. I write a note on the small whiteboard beside my bed, just in case my mom wakes up: *Gone looking for green cows with Simon. Love, Ray.*

We run down the hall, the two of us on the lookout for nurses.

Into the elevator and through the lobby, the fluorescent lights still stinging my eyes. The automatic doors open as we approach, like God himself condones our escape. We get some funny looks as we quicken our pace, the woman at the front desk picking up the phone as we exit the building.

We run across the parking lot, the Red Rocket lighting up like a spaceship. I jump into the front seat and recline back, a panoramic view of the night sky above me. Simon backs up. "We have lift-off," I say.

Simon drives slowly through the parking lot.

"Light speed," he says, jamming down on the accelerator as we reach the street.

I'm staring up at the sky, stars stretched out to infinity, the entire universe spread out before me.

"Faster," I say.

Simon presses down on the accelerator, the minivan lumbering to keep up.

I close my eyes, feel the sensation of weightlessness—no gravity, finally nothing holding me down.

Simon slows down, giving the Red Rocket a break.

"I wish Jane were here," I say.

"Me too," Simon says.

We come to a stop at a traffic light. After a brief pause, Simon says, "Maybe she is here."

"You think?"

"It's not about thinking," Simon says. "It's a feeling."

"I'd like to believe that," I say.

"So what's stopping you?"

Logic, the Scientific Revolution, the Big Bang Theory, the time I watched a TV psychic claim to speak to someone's dead relative who wasn't dead, but had in fact moved to Russia. "I don't know," I say.

Simon puts the car in park, revs the engine. "One more time?"

"Light speed, Scotty," I say.

The light turns green. Simon presses down on the pedal. Green Cow Acres flashes by on our left. The grass cut, the mysteries scorched from the earth, not even a hint of the wild landscape Beddington attempted to tame. I remember standing in the middle of the field, shouting to Jane, finishing our tour of Burgerville on my own. An imaginary future and a confusing past. Is that all I have now?

We go faster and faster, until everything outside the window is just a blur.

I think back to that other piece of Burgerville's history, the piece no amount of perspective or interpretation or research will ever help me understand: Jane waking up in the middle of the night, shaking. The thoughts attacking her: about her dad, about Ellie, about history . . . Or was there something else that set her off that night . . . A fight with her parents? An old picture? Something she took as a sign from a cruel universe? I shake my head. I'll never know. Still, I walk with her to the medicine cabinet. Stand alongside her as she looks at her reflection in the mirror. Watch helplessly as she downs the bottle of pills. I collapse into bed with her too, unable to do anything as her world slowly fades to black.

I take a deep breath. The night closing in on me. The minivan twirling through space and time. Simon to my left. The history of Burgerville, the history of Jane surrounding us.

"You okay, Ray?"

I shake my head. Take another deep breath. "Faster," I say.

"But the speed limit," Simon says. "If I get a ticket . . ."

"What would Jane say?"

That settles the debate.

We approach a hill. Simon steadies his grip on the steering wheel. He turns to me, gives me a look, the type of expression a pilot might give their copilot when making a crash landing. He presses down on the accelerator. The minivan jolts forward, the gears shifting, wheels grinding . . .

"Is that all the Red Rocket's got?"

Simon presses down even harder, his hand on the center console like he's driving stick. The engine sounds like it's about to give out. The jangle of metal makes me worry that the Red Rocket's going to disintegrate mid-flight. I can smell rubber burning, mixing with the crisp spring air rushing in through the window. I keep my gaze focused on the sky, the shaking and rumbling bringing me closer to the moon, to the stars, to Jane. I hold my breath. Trying to break free of that final image of Jane. Her ending.

Almost to the top. A red light blinks on the dashboard, one of those early warning signs that either Simon needs an oil change or the van's about to blow up. But just as I start to worry that we might need to hitchhike back to the hospital, the strangest thing happens.

We reach the top of the hill and miraculously take flight. It's only a moment, but that moment stretches out . . .

And in those few seconds before the tires hit the road, I see the history of Jane Doe clearly. The history of Jane is alive, electric, coursing through the present, woven into every touch, every kiss, every moment we shared together, a delicate tapestry that stretches backward and forward. This moment connected with every moment that came before, with the entire History of Burgerville.

The truth is—and it hits me forcefully in the gut, almost like we've just broken free of the atmosphere and are halfway to the moon—the truth is, the history of Jane can hardly be called history.

The Red Rocket comes crashing down, Simon and I lurching forward, the seat belts catching us as we land and come to a screeching halt in the middle of the road.

Neither one of us speaks. We sit in silence. The sound of crickets grows louder. The moon above—that same moon that's watched history unfold for thousands of years—hangs precariously in the night sky, as if a slight breeze could send it tumbling to the ground.

"Holy shit," Simon says. "Did you see that? I feel like we were at least fifty feet off the ground."

Simon starts to laugh. I join in. He bangs on the steering wheel, honks the horn, and grabs my shoulder. And I swear I can hear Jane laughing too. Asking us to do it again. I close my eyes, try to hold on to that feeling. I imagine seeing her reflection in the rearview mirror. Her eyes gazing up through the moon roof at the sky.

We head back to the hospital. The engine sputters out with a pathetic whine as Simon coasts into the parking lot. He powers down the van, rubbing the top of the dashboard. "Atta girl."

Simon reclines back, so now we're both looking up at the sky.

"What are you thinking about?" Simon asks.

I could tell Simon I'm thinking about Jane. All of the different versions layered over all of the different times of Burgerville. How no matter what, history can never encapsulate a person. How I'm starting to realize that each *what* contains a multitude of *whys*. That history is only a word for academics; it surrounds us, all of the pieces floating in space, able to be built and rebuilt like a game of Jenga.

"I'm thinking about how lucky we are," I say instead.

290 DAYS AFTER

ALL-YOU-CAN-EAT PIZZA AND DRIVE-IN MOVIE THEATERS

For the last year, I've dedicated myself to the *why*. When attempting to do my homework, eating, lying under my comforter wishing the world would disappear: Why? It attached itself to everything I did, everywhere I went, following me around like a shadow; and every time I turned around to chase it, it would disappear.

I can hear Tim and my mom downstairs in the kitchen now. The faint sound of laughter, the smell of chocolate chip cookies rising through the vent in my room. I imagine them huddled closely together, Tim's arm around my mom's shoulder—and I can honestly say that I'm happy for them.

"Ray?" I hear my mom call up the stairs. "Cookies."

"Be right down," I yell.

Maybe I've just gotten bored with staring at the wall all day and writing down my thoughts. But I kind of think we can only tell ourselves so much. At some point we have to shut up, pick the pile of clothes off the floor, and go see what it's like outside.

This morning, I woke up and saw that my petition to change Town Hall had gone viral. Over a thousand signatures in the last couple days, which is like a million in Burgerville-speak. The town council is now considering a vote to change it. "To reflect the true blemishes and blunders of our history," the press release states. Yours truly is even mentioned. Who says you can't change history?

At our last session, I told Rich I had a breakthrough. "Your mental health exercises are no longer needed," I said.

He laughed.

"Why are you laughing?" I asked.

"If you have the secret, would you share it with me so I can tell my other clients?"

"You have a wife and kids, Rich. If people didn't have problems, you'd be living on the street."

"As long as there are people, there will be problems," he said.

I agreed. We sat in silence in Rich's dim office, our two chairs facing each other.

"Do you believe in an afterlife?" I asked.

Rich took a deep breath. "I'm not a priest."

"Not like the one with clouds and naked babies playing harps. I mean the sane people one. You know, just somewhere we go when we die?"

"I don't know," he said. "It would be nice."

I nodded. "Maybe it doesn't matter if it's true or not then. Half the time we're all just making shit up anyway. Why not make up *good* stories? Why shouldn't we go to an all-you-can-eat pizza buffet when we die?"

"Or a drive-in movie theater," Rich said.

"Yeah, or even better, how about a *real* movie theater," I said, trying to help Rich conceptualize a better version of heaven.

The rest of the session we traded alternate versions of our paradise, which somehow always included ridiculous amounts of food, exotic locations, fairies (Rich, not me), and the Beatles (both of us). Of course, the only part I didn't mention to Rich was the one that mattered most, the one I wanted to keep just for me. In every single version, Jane was there.

NOW

NEVER HAD I EVER

Simon picks me up in the Red Rocket.

"What's in the bag?" he says when I jump into the van.

"I'll tell you when we get there."

"Where are we going?"

"Beddington's statue," I say. "Light speed, Scotty."

"Simon. The name's Simon."

I recline back and take in the view through the moon roof. The eternity of the stars dwarves the history of Burgerville.

We arrive at Beddington's statue. I look up at Town Hall, a building designed to emulate the absurdity of the universe. But I imagine the opposite, a world full of meaning, a world with answers to every why and what and how—

Because in an alternative dimension, this is happening:

Jane puts the bottle of pills back in the medicine cabinet.

Her father gets up from his wheelchair.

Ellie's still chasing the Flying Possum of Williamsburg.

And Jane is still Jane. Not some paper cut-out, but the three-dimensional version, what no amount of words could ever do justice to.

Simon snaps his fingers in front of my face, waking me up from my daydream.

"Why are we here?" Simon asks.

"That's a great question," I say. I know he means at Beddington's statue, but I can't help but think of it in the cosmic sense. Why are we here? In this place and time? In this town? And of course, the opposite: Why isn't Jane here?

A question with a thousand different answers, each depending on what dimension you find yourself in.

When someone dies, we spend so much time looking for an explanation. The rest of the time we spend making sure we won't forget them. So we build statues. Hold memorials. Visit graves. All of these physical markers that make it impossible to forget. But what if it's the opposite? What if the only way we can really remember is if we stop looking to the past? Maybe then they'll become more them and less us.

I feel like I can finally remember how Jane used to smirk. And then smile. Almost like she was hiding it. How she'd roll her eyes, but in a way that made you want her to do it again. The first time I saw her. Our first kiss at Beddington's party. All of the many different versions of Jane, existing in moments, perfectly preserved. No spin or interpretation, just Jane. The historian is finally out of the picture. The past is now just the past. The amazing, complicated, tragic, beautiful, fantastic past.

I turn to Simon, who has just finished taking a selfie that makes it look like Beddington's giving him a high five.

"I think I finally know how to say good-bye," I say.

I zip open the bag, pass Simon a gallon of milk, and take out a small bottle of whiskey I stole from my mom's liquor cabinet.

"Do you have whole?" Simon says.

I shoot him a look.

"Okay, two percent will do."

Simon opens his milk, takes a swig.

"Hold on," I say. I take a deep breath and unscrew the cap. "Before Jane . . . Never had I ever kissed a girl." I take a sip.

"Before Jane . . . Never had I ever had a girl think I was funny," Simon says. "You know? Not weird funny. But actually funny." He chugs the milk.

"Never had I ever been so happy that I thought my heart might explode," I say. I take hold of my chest. "Sometimes it still hurts."

Simon holds up the bottle of milk to the sky. "Never had I ever felt like I was part of something, like I was at the lunch table where people wanted to sit. And not just because they wanted to steal my food. But because they wanted to hang out with me."

We both drink, holding up our bottles to the universe, acolytes proffering the one thing we still have: our memories.

"Never had I ever felt so sad," I say. "But the good kind of sad. The kind that means you really care about something. The kind that means you have something to lose."

"I didn't know how much we were missing out on," Simon says. He takes a sip, wipes his milk mustache.

"No one does," I say.

We keep going, sip after sip, until my head is spinning.

We walk over to the statue. I read the inscription at the base: *Visionaries don't see with their eyes, they see with their hearts.*

"Jane," I whisper, my head tilted toward the sky.

Simon and I sit down with our backs to the statue, Beddington's arms overhead, forever reaching, never wavering in his belief in what he saw.

I lay my head back on the marble, content with the knowledge that maybe, just maybe, there's a green cow running around in Green Cow Acres, and the moon really does change history, and the ghost of McCallen is still treating patients from beyond the grave. And Jane is somewhere—call it heaven, call it whatever you want—making sarcastic comments about all those harps, complaining about the softness of the clouds, and telling Ellie all about Burgerville, a place more unbelievable than anything likely to be found behind the pearly gates.

AUTHOR'S NOTE

Talking about mental illness can sometimes feel like a riddle. It's omnipresent but invisible. The people who need the most help are often the least likely to ask. It makes you feel completely alone even though, according to the National Alliance on Mental Illness, approximately 1 in 5 teenagers and adults live with a mental health condition.

I grew up in the shadow of my grandmother's depression, similar to Jane's experience with her grandma Irene. My grandfather dedicated much of his life to supporting my grandmother as she fought this faceless enemy, but unlike fairy tales, the dragon was never slayed. There were bad moments—suicide attempts, time spent in mental hospitals, weeks where she'd stay in bed. But those shadows are tiny compared to how much light she brought into our lives.

I didn't really get it growing up, and I can't say I fully get it now. But that's the thing about mental illness; there's the diagnosis, and then there's the experience, a pain that's often indescribable, much to the confusion of family and friends. As Rich tells Ray, "Depression is like this black light on everything in your life so you can only see the bad stuff." How do you help someone fight demons you can't see?

It's easy to feel haunted by mental illness, whether because of a loved one or your own struggles with depression and anxiety.

I've been there, and some days I'm still there, though I've been lucky enough to be given some flashlights along the way. There are no quick fixes—no random images, folk songs, or affirmations that will magically erase the pain—but there are ways to live with mental illness, manage it, and even conquer it.

If you or someone you know needs help, don't be afraid to ask. There's an entire village of people who care—friends, family, teachers, guidance counselors, school nurses, and therapists like Rich. For help finding a mental health professional, call the Substance Abuse and Mental Health Services Administration's National Helpline (1-800-662-4357). If you're feeling at risk of suicide and don't know who else to turn to, please call the National Suicide Prevention Lifeline (1-800-273-8255). Your life matters. The world can't stand to lose another John or Jane Doe.

ACKNOWLEDGMENTS

The history of *The History of Jane Doe* could probably fill its own volume, but like Roger Lutz says, that's the problem with history; there's always too much of it. With that in mind, I'll keep my acknowledgments brief. At least I'll try.

First, I have to thank the Westport Writers' Workshop for giving me a place to hone my craft and meet other like-minded writers. My first workshop in the fall of 2014—the same workshop where I shared the beginning of *THOJD* (is it presumptuous to make my book an acronym?)—completely changed my life. To have a community of fellow writers critiquing and celebrating my work—especially Katie Agis, Heather Frimmer, Denitza Krasteva, Kate Marlow, Paul McCarthy, and Loretto Leary—is a gift I will always be thankful for.

I was beyond lucky to have Chris Belden as a workshop leader during my time at WWW, and now even luckier to call him both a mentor and friend. Chris offered invaluable feedback on the manuscript and encouraged me to send it out to agents. He also came up with the greatest pitch of all time when he called the book a cross between *The Catcher in the Rye* and *The Simpsons*. I would not be the writer I am today without Chris's support.

I'm also forever indebted to my agent, Stephanie Fretwell-Hill, who took a chance on a manuscript written by someone with no actual writing credentials. Of course, the great paradox of publishing is that you can only get credentials by publishing, which often seems akin to winning the lottery or being the first person to discover a new species. At least that's what it feels like after each new rejection. But like Earl Beddington, Stephanie believed in Burgerville's green cows right from the beginning.

Many thanks to my editor, Kate Harrison, who was able to sort through all the history of Burgerville and help me find the true heart of the story. Every writer needs a champion, someone willing to keep pushing them, let them fail and veer off into ridiculous territory as they attempt to navigate a world filled with strange history and flying possums—and Kate Harrison is that person for me. Her insights brought Jane's story to life, and her dedication to the book gave me the confidence I needed to see it through. Words cannot express how grateful I am to have found an editor who believes in Burgerville as much as I do.

I'm also honored to be working with the amazing team at Dial and Penguin Random House. Writing can often feel like a solitary pursuit, but that's not the case with publishing. Thank you to Lauri Hornik and Ellen Cormier for their suggestions on the manuscript, Regina Castillo for her copyediting talents and magic with tenses, Dana Li and Jasmin Rubero for a book design that perfectly reflects Ray's search for answers and Burgerville's bizarre past, and Bridget Hartzler for helping Ray and Jane's story find its audience. I couldn't ask for a better home for *The History of Jane Doe*.

Thank you also to Grace Lee for bringing the world of Burgerville to life with her whimsical illustrations. It's such a thrill to see people and places that have lived in my head for the past few years be translated so beautifully onto the page.

Thank you to Dr. Jennifer Hartstein for her helpful feedback on the therapist/client relationship, especially her thoughts on how a therapist would approach a topic as complicated and delicate as suicide. Thank you as well to the various mental health practitioners who have provided a safe and supportive environment for me to do my own version of what Rich euphemistically calls "Brain Cleaning." I would not be where I am today without the help of these caring professionals.

Thanks to Fairfield University's MFA program for helping me grow as a writer and providing an inspiring place to disappear to during ten wonderful days in the summer and winter. Thank you to Al Davis, Sonya Huber, Eugenia Kim, Karen Osborn, Hollis Seamon, Michael White, and all of my colleagues for everything they've taught me about writing and the creative process.

I'm also grateful to Fairfield University's American Studies program for allowing me to write my first novel as my master's thesis. Though the novel lives in my closet, the experience lives on in my heart, as do a thousand other clichés. Special thanks to Nicholas Rinaldi for being the first person to ever say the most magical four words in the English language: "You are a writer."

And I think that's it.

Your family. You're forgetting your family.

Of course! Thank you to my family for reading early drafts of the novel and being genuinely enthusiastic about it (or lying to protect my feelings), taking my ambitions to be a writer seriously, and occasionally comparing me to their favorite authors. Mom, Dad, Megan, Matt, Amanda, Andrea, Hammy, Bella, and even Mojo (my parents' chi-corgi who seems to believe I'm the devil incarnate): I'm honored to share my genes with such amazing people (and dogs).

Thank you to Emily Hernberg for letting me bother her to read scenes throughout all of the twists and turns of the revision process. I couldn't ask for a better partner, best friend, and podcast buddy. Thanks also to Louisa and Laura, our two cats, whose punny names befit two cat people who love literature: Louisa May Alcatt and Laura Ingalls Wildcat. It's probably already been done before, and I don't want to ruin the illusion of originality by googling, so I'll just pretend we were first.

Now for closure, a buzzword every teacher knows well, and a fitting way to end the acknowledgments for a book that grew partly out of my experiences teaching high school. Thank you to everyone who has made my day job so rewarding. Thank you to my colleagues for their encouragement and guidance, especially the inspirational pep talks after the lessons that just didn't go my way. I know how you feel, Mr. Parker. And thank you to my students for teaching me what bravery really is. Day after day, I'm inspired by your strength and perseverance. Studying for a test on the Great Depression even though you're struggling with your own depression. Revising an essay while your parents fight in the next room. Creating supply and demand graphs after losing a loved one only a short while ago. Be brave, but remember to ask for help.

MICHAEL BELANGER (@MBelanger514) is a debut young adult author and high school history teacher. He is a member of the Westport Writers' Workshop and faculty advisor to *Greenwitch*, a high school literary magazine that has published talented young writers—including Truman Capote—for over one hundred years. He currently lives in Connecticut.